RIDING TO THE MOON

Riding to the Moon

BY

Barbara Cartland

New York EVEREST HOUSE *Publishers*

Copyright © 1982 by Barbara Cartland
All Rights Reserved
Published by Everest House
33 West 60th Street, New York, N. Y. 10023
Published simultaneously in Canada by
Beaverbooks, Pickering, Ontario
Manufactured in the United States of America
First Edition   FG882

LIBRARY OF CONGRESS CATALOGING IN PUBLICATION DATA:

Cartland, Barbara, 1902–
    Riding to the moon.

    I. Title.
PR6005.A765R5   1982   823'.912   82-10198
ISBN 0-89696-174-5

AUTHOR'S NOTE

Steeple-Chases were inspired by the hell-for-leather match races run all through the ages, across any naturally fenced country which was available. The winner proved that he could get his horse from one place to another faster than anyone else.

During the Regency it became fashionable to have private Steeple-Chases, and this involved erecting special fences and marking out a course with flags.

Steeple-Chasing was popular with sportsmen from its very beginning but was frowned on by the established authorities of flat racing.

The most famous Steeple-Chase in the world—the Grand National—started in 1839. It was four miles across country, with twenty-nine jumps, and the purse was twelve hundred pounds.

The poems quoted in this novel come from *Shih Ching*, the first anthology of Chinese poetry, about 561 – 579 B.C., and from the T'ang Dynasty, 618 – 907 A.D.

C.2

Chapter One

THE Morning-Room at White's Club was rapidly filling up with its aristocratic members, both famous and infamous.

The Bow window looking onto St. James's Street, which Beau Brummell had made famous, was already full, and there was not a brown leather chair available when Lord Frodham and his friend Sir James Overton walked into the room.

They stopped to talk to a friend with whom they had spent the previous evening, and as they did so they heard a voice say:

"You are becoming as boring as George Byron on the subject of love, which I can assure you is nothing but desire tied up with pretty ribbons."

There was laughter at this, and Charles Frodham said in a low voice to Jimmy Overton:

"Ardsley, at his most cynical! I have always believed he was crossed in love when he was young."

"Nonsense!" Jimmy Overton replied. "He has never been in love with anybody except himself and his horses!"

Charles Frodham laughed, and moved a little nearer to the Bow window to hear what else the Marquis of Ardsley had to say on the subject.

Somebody was obviously arguing with him, and he said scathingly:

"Women have two uses—to amuse and to produce the necessary heir. Otherwise, a man of any intelligence has other interests to fill his life."

"That is all very well, Ardsley," a notorious Rake

exclaimed. "But you know as well as I do that life would be very dull and colourless without pretty women in our arms and in our bed."

"There speaks the expert!" somebody exclaimed, and there was a roar of laughter.

"Every man to his own taste," the Marquis replied, when he could make himself heard. "At the same time, I was reading this morning that poor Oliver Markham has made a damned fool of himself, and somebody ought to have warned him."

"You mean that he should not have married an heiress?" the Rake asked incredulously. "It is all very well for you to sneer at money, Ardsley, but those of us who have pockets to let know that it is the only way we can keep up our ancestral homes and put decent horses in our stables."

"There are heiresses and heiresses," the Marquis said coldly. "Do you not realise that Markham has married the daughter of a tradesman?"

The scathing condemnation in his voice was almost like the bite of a cold wind.

"Perhaps he had no other choice," somebody ventured.

"Nonsense!" the Marquis said. "Markham comes from a very old family, and, thank God, blue blood and a respected title still have their established value in the Social Marriage Market. He has been a fool, and I shall not hesitate to tell him so."

"It is too late, Ardsley," the Rake said. "He is married, and doubtless we shall all be delighted to be asked to the parties which Oliver will give! Personally, I have always been very fond of him."

"And fonder still, now that he can afford to entertain you," somebody said mockingly.

"I blame myself and you too," the Marquis said in a serious tone. "When we realised that Oliver was serious in pursuing this unspeakable creature, we should have prevented him from marrying her."

"I heard," another man said tentatively, who had not spoken before, "that she is very attractive, and that Markham is in love with her."

"Love! Love!" the Marquis exclaimed. "Now we are back to that nonsensical emotion all over again! Let me make it quite clear: where marriage is concerned, love is the least important consideration to any man who has any sense."

"Like yourself!" the Rake mocked.

"Of course," the Marquis answered. "When I marry, which will not be for many years, I shall choose somebody with a pedigree to equal my own, and who will not offend me or shame the position she will hold as my wife by her low-class manners and low-class ideas."

"You are quite certain you would recognise her for what she is?" somebody asked.

"If I did not know a Thoroughbred when I saw one, I would give up racing," the Marquis answered sharply, "and I can assure you it is easier to detect the finer points of a woman than of a horse."

There was silence for a moment. Then someone asked:

"Are you telling me, Ardsley, that just as you claim you are an expert on horse-breeding, you can tell how a woman, or a man for that matter, is bred when you meet them, without a form-book to guide you?"

"Of course I can," the Marquis said positively. "However pretty, however attractive, however good an actress a woman might be, I can assure you I am never deceived."

"I would like to have a bet with you on that," the Rake said, "but as I have the uncomfortable feeling I would lose my money, I shall not ask for the Betting-Book."

The Betting-Book at White's was one of its most famous possessions.

Since 1743 members had entered their bets in the book, which was kept in a safe place in the Club, and which thereby became a sacred commitment on which no member would welsh.

Some of the bets were serious, but many were frivolous.

Births and marriages were almost as popular subjects for bets as death: "Would Lord E. marry Lady B.'s daughter in duty-bound?" "Was Lady C. in the family way?"

Lord Eglington in 1757 made a bet that he would find a man who could kill twenty snipe in three-and-twenty shots, and Lord Alington on a wet day bet three thousand pounds on which of two raindrops would first get to the bottom of a pane of glass.

During the war with France, Wellington's campaigns provided material for innumerable wagers, and many of the members believed firmly in Napoleon's invincibility, only to lose their money.

As the Rake finished speaking, Charles Frodham looked at Jimmy Overton; then, because they knew what each other was thinking, they walked away from the Bow window to the far end of the Morning-Room and sat down to order a drink before Charles Frodham said:

"Do you think anybody would lay us twenty-to-one on his being deceived sooner or later?"

"Not a chance!" Jimmy Overton replied. "I expect what he says is the truth, and no woman could take him in."

"I do not believe it," Charles remarked. "Women are born actresses, and if we could find one who was as clever off the stage as Madame Vestris is on, she could lead him up the garden-path and make a fool of him."

"I would love to see that," Jimmy replied. "He gets under my skin because he is so damned pleased with himself. But I am sure he is like a fox-hound on the scent and would know an imposter before she could even open her mouth."

"You are as bad as he is!" Charles said crossly. "And because I intend to prove to you how wrong you are, I will find a woman somewhere, and I will bet you one hundred guineas that Ardsley will be unaware she is not *crème de la crème* for at least three days after he has met her."

"Done!" Jimmy answered. "But you have to play fair."

"That is what I should be saying to you," Charles protested. "I do not trust you to avoid losing one hundred guineas. How do I know you will not tip off Ardsley so that you will win?"

"Now you are insulting me," Jimmy cried, "and if you are not careful I will call you out and drill a hole through you!"

"You have no more chance of doing that," Charles laughed, "than of making Ardsley apologise when we prove him wrong."

"That is something I would really enjoy!"

"I do not like Ardsley," Charles said. "He is always laying down the law about women, and if you ask me, it takes away some of the enjoyment we have in them, which is exactly what he intends."

"I too dislike Ardsley, and I always have," his friend replied. "At the same time, I have to admit that he is a 'top-notcher' when it comes to sport, and his horses are better than anybody else's."

"So are his women, whatever he thinks about them," Charles agreed. "If you want the truth, I will never forgive him for taking Clarice away from me."

"I can understand that," Jimmy said sympathetically. "She was lovely! Quite the most alluring 'bit o' muslin' you ever pursued."

"Hopelessly, thanks to Ardsley!" Charles exclaimed bitterly. "That is why I would like to get even with him. If I could find another Clarice, and convince him that her blood was as blue as his, he would not only have to eat his words, but he would look damned foolish when we revealed that she was actually straight out of the gutter."

Jimmy put back his head and laughed.

"Really, Charles, you are crazy to have such ideas. You know as well as I do that any woman who is as lovely and as fascinating as Clarice is quite certainly not going to be accepted at Richmond House, nor by any other of the great hostesses. Ardsley may think he can detect a social imposter, but no-one is more astute than other women."

"That is true," Charles admitted. "My grandmother has every debutante's pedigree at her fingertips and scrutinises them through a magnifying-glass before she offers them to me as prospective brides."

"I am sorry for you! Your grandmother frightens me, and I do not know how you have managed to evade matrimony for so long."

"It has been difficult at times," Charles admitted, "and I expect I shall eventually be caught."

There was silence for a moment between the two friends. Then Jimmy said:

"Well, what about having luncheon and forgetting this rather gloomy discourse?"

"Certainly not!" Charles said sharply. "I am going to call for the Betting-Book and record our bet in it."

"Do not mention Ardsley by name."

"No, of course not," Charles replied. "I am not as bird-witted as that."

He raised his hand, and instantly a steward came to his side.

"The Betting-Book."

"Very good, M'Lord."

The leather-bound book was brought and set down at Charles Frodham's side, together with an ink-pot and a quill-pen.

Charles thought for a moment before he wrote carefully:

1st *May* 1818.
Lord Frodham bets Sir James Overton that he will deceive a certain nobleman for three days without his being aware of it.

"Is that ambiguous enough?" Charles asked.

"It will make everybody who reads it damned curious," Jimmy replied.

"It will give them something to think about," Charles said with a grin. "Come on, let us go up to the Coffee-Room."

He put down the pen and the steward carried the Betting-Book away. Then the two friends started to wend their way through the Morning-Room, which had grown fuller still since they had been talking.

They had just reached the door when a voice behind them said:

"Frodham! Overton! I wanted to see you! I am running a Steeple-Chase and I would like you both to take part in it."

The eyes of both the young men lit up.

The Marquis's Steeple-Chases were famous, not only because they were well run and most enjoyable, but also because the house-parties he gave with them at Ardsley Hall were legendary. An invitation to one of them was more prized than one to Carlton House or the Royal Pavilion at Brighton.

"Thank you very much," Charles Frodham said before his friend could speak. "Jimmy and I will look forward to it."

"Send your horses on ahead of you," the Marquis said carelessly, "to give them a chance to rest before the big event, and I shall expect you both on Thursday night. The race will take place on Saturday, and I expect there will be a lot of competitors."

"I am sure there will be," Charles said. "I have a new horse which might even defeat Your Lordship's."

The Marquis laughed.

"You can try," he said, "but I shall be extremely annoyed if my new one, which I have not yet tried out, is not the victor."

He walked away as he spoke, supremely sure of himself and moving through the Club in a majestic manner that invariably aroused a respect that other men were not accorded.

Charles and Jimmy went upstairs to the Coffee-Room

and sat down at a table in the window where they could be alone.

"Do you really think you have a chance of beating the Marquis?" Jimmy asked.

"I said that to annoy him," Charles admitted. "I expect he will win, he always does."

"That is what is so intensely irritating!" Jimmy agreed. "I know my horses have not a chance against his, but I shall enjoy the Steeple-Chase and also the party. I wonder who will be there."

"Beauties galore," Charles said casually.

"Somebody told me last night that the Marquis actually danced with Lady Beris at Richmond House," Jimmy said, "and the Duke had visions of having him as a son-in-law."

Charles laughed.

"Not a chance! He spends his time, I am told, with a new charmer—Lady Sinclair—although I doubt if she will hold him for long."

"The Countess of Martindale is one of the prettiest women I have ever seen," Jimmy said. "Ardsley dropped her in a month, so how are you going to find a 'gutter-snipe' to compete with her?"

"I will find someone," Charles said confidently. "But not a gutter-snipe. I think she will have to be an actress."

"That will cost you a pretty penny."

"I shall have your hundred guineas towards expenses."

"I have never before made a bet I have been so certain of winning," Jimmy answered provocatively.

"I think it only fair that just for once he should be in the wrong," Charles said as if he was speaking to himself.

He was frowning as he spoke, and Jimmy knew he was still feeling angry at the way in which the Marquis had swept Clarice away from him in a high-handed manner that would have annoyed anybody, especially Charles Frodham.

Very good-looking, wealthy because his father had died while he was still a minor, and the owner of a very charming if not particularly impressive Estate in Huntingdonshire, Charles was run after by the most attractive women in the *Beau Monde* and courted by ambitious mothers for their young daughters.

He had good grounds for being conceited and proud of himself, but it was no use pretending that he was not e-clipsed by the Marquis of Ardsley.

Jimmy Overton was not ambitious and was quite content to be only comparatively well off. Yet, he had enough money to enjoy himself in London and to keep up the delightful Seventeenth-Century Manor he owned in Essex.

As his mother ran it very competently and was in no hurry to move to the Dower House, he was not pestered as his friend was to settle down and get married.

He had therefore every intention of enjoying himself and remaining free for a great number of years before he asked any woman, however attractive or suitable, to be his wife.

Because he and Charles had been close friends at Eton and at Oxford, they enjoyed life together, hunting as a couple, being welcomed not only by the great hostesses at every Ball, Reception, and Assembly, but also by the Madams in the "Houses of Pleasure" and the Dance-Halls, where the prettiest "Cyprians" ran towards them with open arms.

Jimmy knew that Charles's pride had certainly been bruised if not deflated by the way in which the Marquis had taken the lovely Clarice from him at the very moment when he was considering setting her up in a small house in Chelsea and taking her officially under his protection.

"What are you thinking about?" Jimmy asked now.

"The pleasure I shall enjoy at seeing Ardsley discomfited."

"You cannot say that until you have found this paragon who I am convinced does not exist," Jimmy said practically.

"I will prove him wrong if it is the last thing I do!" Charles said aggressively.

Jimmy laughed as he said:

"Actually, I would willingly pay five hundred guineas to see Ardsley 'bite the dust,' which is strange when you think about it, because he has never done me any harm."

"It is insufferable that any man should walk about as if he were God!"

"That is rather a good description," Jimmy said. "At the same time, the sort of god you really mean is the fellow we read about at Oxford—what was he called?—the one who drives his Chariot across the sky by day."

"Apollo."

"That is right."

"We saw a statue of him when we were in Rome, and Ardsley does look like him," Charles remarked.

"That is the answer, then," Jimmy said. "He is Apollo, a god, and we poor devils are just humans."

"Even gods, if my mythology is not at fault," Charles said, "were susceptible to pretty women, but I have the uncomfortable feeling that it was the male gods who disguised themselves, rather than the goddesses."

"Oh, well, you can rewrite the whole of Greek—or was it Roman?—mythology to suit yourself," Jimmy said with a smile, "but Apollo or no Apollo, I am hungry."

*

It was a week later when Lord Frodham and Sir James Overton set off from Charles's house in the country to drive to Ardsley Hall.

Their horses had left two days earlier, both gentlemen having given their grooms strict instructions to take them easily and to make sure that they were in perfect condition for the Steeple-Chase on Saturday.

Besides thinking of his horses, Charles had given a great deal of his time to searching for a young actress with whom he intended to deceive the Marquis into believing that she was as blue-blooded as he was.

"If you are going to give her a fictitious name," Jimmy said, "you will have to be careful to choose one of which the Marquis will not be suspicious. I am quite certain he knows the genealogical tree of every family in the country."

"That is the least of our worries," Charles said after the third day and night of searching the Theatres and Dance-Halls and even the "Houses of Pleasure" for a likely candidate.

Once or twice they had seen a face that was so attractive and so pretty that Charles had thought his search was at an end.

But the beauty in question had only to open her mouth to betray an accent that no possible amount of tuition could disguise from anybody as astute as the Marquis.

"Of course, we may have to teach her how to speak," Charles conceded, "but perhaps if she was a foreigner it would be easier."

"I have always been told that the Marquis of Ardsley is very good at languages," Jimmy said. "In fact, I remember hearing that he has helped Lord Hawkesley at the Foreign Office on various occasions."

Charles's lips tightened, but he made no comment, and they moved on to look elsewhere for a creature who Jimmy was already convinced was as rare as a dodo-bird.

Jimmy actually had found the chase most enjoyable, although he was sorry for his friend, and now as they drove through the countryside at a spanking pace behind Charles's team of bays he said:

"I ought to have insisted that we have a time-limit on our wager, otherwise I can see us spending the rest of our summer searching for the unobtainable, with you growing more and more grumpy in the process."

"I am not grumpy," Charles replied, "and I have not given up hope! But I have begun to think that we are looking in the wrong places."

"What do you mean by that?"

"The sort of woman we want is more likely to be found in the country than in London. You know as well as I do that if she was beautiful enough for our requirements, she would have been snapped up the moment she set foot in one of those overcrowded Dance-Halls. And if she was on the Stage, her dressing-room would be full of followers."

"You certainly have something there," Jimmy replied, "and I was just thinking that when I was young, the Vicar of the family Church to which I was taken every Sunday had an extremely pretty daughter."

Charles turned from his contemplation of the road ahead to look at his friend and ask:

"Where is she now?"

Jimmy laughed as he replied:

"Married, with a large family!"

"Then why the hell are you talking about her?"

"I was only agreeing with you that pretty girls are not the prerogative of London."

"If they are pretty enough, it is the one place they want to go."

"That is true," Jimmy agreed. "So what you have to do, Charles, is to trap 'em before they get there!"

"You are laughing at me," Charles said, "and so damned sure of taking my hundred guineas off me that you are getting as bad as Ardsley himself!"

Jimmy sighed as he said:

"I want to topple him off his perch! At the same time, I am quite prepared to eat his superlative food, stay in the most comfortable house in England, and applaud him as he wins the first prize at his own Steeple-Chase."

"If you say one more word," Charles threatened, "I will turn you out of the Phaeton and make you walk."

"In these Hessians?" Jimmy exclaimed. "For God's sake, Charles, it would be a Chinese Torture!"

They both laughed as they drove on.

The sunshine, which had been somewhat fitful earlier in the day, had now disappeared behind dark clouds.

Then, after luncheon in a comfortable Inn, where Charles changed his team of bays for four perfectly matched chestnuts, the sky was not only overcast but there were rumbles of thunder in the distance.

"Damn!" Charles said irritably. "We are going to get wet. I should have thought of travelling in my fastest Chariot so that we could put the hood up."

"It will be very unpleasant to arrive looking like a drowned rat," Jimmy said reflectively. "I am quite certain that the Marquis, if he were in our place, would manage to control the elements."

"I agree with you, but there seems to be nothing we can do about it, and we still have at least another hour's driving before we get there."

Ardsley Hall was in Hampshire, and now, too late, Charles thought that if they had started earlier in the morning, they might have reached their destination before the storm broke.

A sudden flash of forked lightning made the horses nervous, and as he was not certain that if the lightning grew worse, the comparatively young team would not panic, he said:

"There is an Inn about half-a-mile from here. I have never been there, and I expect it is rather scruffy, but it might be wise to take shelter. I do not believe the storm will last long."

"I think you are wise," Jimmy said. "I have heard of nasty accidents taking place in thunderstorms."

As he spoke, he was thinking that four horses were difficult to control at the best of times, and although Charles was an extremely good and experienced driver, he was not a Corinthian like the Marquis.

However, it was something he was far too tactful to say

aloud, and as the lightning flashed again and the crash that followed it seemed nearer than it had been before, he was thankful when Charles drove into the courtyard of an attractive old black-and-white Inn with diamond-paned windows.

The groom clambered down from the back seat and began to give orders to the ostlers who came running from the stables.

Charles put down the reins and climbed from the Phaeton while Jimmy descended on the other side of it.

They walked into the very low-ceilinged Inn, and a large, fat man who was obviously the Landlord came hurrying towards them, wiping his hands on his apron.

"Good-evening, Sirs, you're very welcome!"

"I am Lord Fordham," Charles replied, "and I and my friend will be staying for the duration of the storm. We would like a private Parlour."

"I'm afraid it's small, M'Lord, but it's all we've got," the Landlord replied.

He led the way through an open Lounge in which a large log fire was burning to where at the far end it had obviously been divided by a somewhat makeshift wall of panelling that did not match the rest of the room.

The Parlour was small, as he had said, but there was a fireplace, two armchairs, and a table on which fastidious guests who did not wish to mix with the hoi-polloi could eat in private.

The Landlord bent down to light the fire, and Charles said:

"Bring me a bottle of your best claret. I presume you have no champagne?"

"Afraid not, M'Lord," the Landlord replied, "but th' claret's good, and the brandy, which be French, be very good indeed!"

The way he spoke made it quite clear that the brandy had come across the Channel and no Duty had been paid on it.

"Bring a bottle of both," Charles ordered.

Bowing, with a gratified expression on his face, the Landlord left the room.

There was a small window which looked onto an untidy piece of ground which could hardly be described as a garden, and Jimmy walked towards it.

As he did so there was a flash f lightning which illuminated both the outside and the inside of the Inn, followed by a resounding crash of thunder, and he started back almost as if he had been struck.

"Thank God we are out of this!" Charles exclaimed. "The horses would go mad!"

"We were only just in time," Jimmy agreed. "Another few minutes and we would have been drenched."

Almost as if it were an echo, as he spoke they heard a woman's voice say on the other side of the wall:

"My carriage and horses are drenched. May I stay here until the storm has abated?"

It was a soft, rather attractive voice, and Jimmy thought that in some strange way she sounded a little frightened.

"Yes, of course, Ma'am," he heard the Landlord reply. "Perhaps you'll sit by the fire? And can I offer you a cup o' tea? I feel sure you'd not take wine."

"No, no, of course not," the woman replied, "and a cup of tea would be very pleasant. Thank you."

"I'll see to it at once, Ma'am."

As the Landlord finished speaking he opened the door of the private Parlour and came in carrying a bottle of French brandy and one of claret.

He also had a tray in his hands with four glasses on it, and he set everything down on the table, saying as he did so:

"It's an ill wind that doesn't blow a Landlord some good. I weren't expectin' any visitors today."

He drew the cork from the brandy bottle and as he put it down on the tray Jimmy said:

"I heard you talking to a lady."

The Landlord looked at him, then said in such a low voice that it was almost a whisper:

"A Nun, Sir!"

"A Nun!" Jimmy exclaimed.

The Landlord nodded.

"I wondered why you were so certain she would not take wine," Charles said. "Now I understand."

"It's not often we sees Nuns in this part of the world, M'Lord, and driving in a smart carriage with two horses."

As he opened the bottle of claret the Inn-Keeper added:

"If there's anything else you gentlemen wants, let me know."

"We will," Charles replied.

He walked to the table, poured out half-a-glass of claret, sniffed it, then tasted it tentatively.

"Not bad!"

"I prefer brandy," Jimmy said, "but not too much. As you know, Ardsley's cellar is famous, and I am keeping myself for dinner."

"If we ever get there!" Charles reacted.

The thunder was still deafening overhead, and the rain seemed to increase until the ground outside looked like a pond.

It was such a depressing sight that Jimmy walked to the fire.

"It is overhead," he said, "and I have no wish to endure more than an hour of this."

"Nor have I," Charles agreed. "We are fortunate that when the storm started we were so near to a place of shelter, whatever it might have been like."

"Thank God for it."

As Jimmy spoke he sat down in a comfortable armchair, and his friend sat opposite him.

Because it was hard to make their voices heard above the noise of the rain, they both were silent, sipping their drinks and feeling sleepy from the warmth of the fire.

They had been sitting quietly for quite some time when suddenly there was the sound of a door opening noisily, footsteps, then a cry from the woman they had heard earlier.

It was a cry of fear, and they heard a man's voice saying:

"So here you are! What the hell do you mean by running away and being dressed up like that?"

"I . . . I am going . . . into a . . . Convent . . . and nothing you can . . . say will . . . stop me!"

"I've a great deal to say, and you'll listen to me!"

The man's voice was rough, and although it was educated, there was something about it which told Charles and Jimmy that he was not a gentleman.

"You've put me to a lot of inconvenience," the man said, "and as soon as this storm is over, I'm taking you to London, where you'll do as I tell you."

"If you think I have any intention of marrying Lord Bredon or obeying you in any other way, you are very much mistaken!"

"You'll do as you are told!" the man said sharply. "You ought to be grateful to me, instead of behaving in this mad-cap manner. Going into a Convent indeed! I've never heard of such a thing! Besides, they might not want you."

"I have every intention of becoming a Nun, and they will be only too pleased to accept me . . . and my . . . fortune!"

"So that's your idea, is it? Well, you'll not give your fortune over to any Convent while I'm in charge of you."

"In charge of me?" the woman replied scornfully. "You are not in charge of me. You were employed by my father as his Solicitor, and he would not engage you for a day more if he were still alive."

There was a little tremor in her voice as she said the last word, and Charles and Jimmy, who were listening with undisguised curiosity, thought her father's death must have taken place quite recently.

It was almost as if they were in the audience at one of the

melodramatic plays which held spell-bound those who paid to see them.

"Now listen to me, Mr. Jacobson," the woman said, and it was obvious from her voice that she was young and, Charles was sure, frightened. "I will pay you anything you ask, even if it is a large sum, when I am twenty-one and have control of my fortune."

The man laughed, and it was not a pleasant sound.

"Do you really think I am going to wait for three years? Lord Bredon has promised me ten thousand pounds the day he marries you—and the sooner the better, from his point of view and yours."

"What do you mean . . . and mine? I will not marry . . . Lord Bredon. I hate him . . . as I hate all men . . . and I do not . . . intend to . . . marry anybody!"

For a moment it seemed that Mr. Jacobson was stunned before he said:

"You've got bats in your belfry, that's what you've got! All women want to get married, and Bredon's a gentleman all right, and you'll look pretty in a coronet."

"I daresay he has pawned that with everything else," the woman said scornfully. "If you think I want to marry a bankrupt to save him from being taken to the Fleet Prison as a debtor, you are the one who is mad! Papa would be appalled by your behaviour."

"Your father's dead and there's nothing you can do about it," Mr. Jacobson said roughly. "And if it's not Lord Bredon, it will be another fortune-hunter of some sort, and you'll find there is not much to choose between any of them."

"I am not going to choose. As I have already told you, I am going into a Convent, and there is nothing you can do to stop me."

Mr. Jacobson laughed.

"That's what you think! You will come to London with me willingly, or I'll take you unconscious. That's the only choice you've got. What's more, we're going now, and if you get wet, you've only yourself to blame."

"I will not . . . come with you . . . I will not!"

Her defiant words ended in a scream, and Charles and Jimmy knew that she was fighting against Mr. Jacobson, who was dragging her towards the door.

They looked at each other and without saying anything rose to their feet.

They put down their glasses and, pulling open the Parlour door, walked out into the Lounge.

As they both expected, Mr. Jacobson, an unpleasant, foxy-looking man, was dragging the woman towards the outer door of the Inn.

She was resisting in every way possible, but she was small while he was large, and there was no doubt how the contest would end.

In the struggle the woman's veil had fallen off, and Charles, who had walked out first, had a glimpse of thick red tresses falling over her black-draped shoulders before he punched Mr. Jacobson hard with his clenched fist.

The Solicitor immediately released the woman's wrist and put up his own hands.

But he was too late.

Charles hit him again, this time on the chin, and he fell to the ground, out for the count.

Jimmy turned from the satisfaction he was receiving from watching his friend in action, to see two very large eyes looking up at him and hear a voice say fervently:

"Oh, thank you . . . thank you!"

He was just thinking that she was one of the prettiest girls he had ever seen in his life, when Charles turned round.

"What shall I do about him now?" he asked.

The girl, for she was nothing more, was looking apprehensively at Mr. Jacobson lying unconscious on the floor.

"I . . . I must get . . . away!" she said, "but the horse . . . that . . . brought me here from Southampton is very tired . . . and I am afraid that when he revives, Mr. Jacobson will . . . catch up with me . . . again."

Charles looked at Jimmy and smiled.

"I think we can prevent that from happening."

"Of course!" Jimmy replied.

As he spoke he looked round and saw that there was a heavy curtain that could be pulled over the outer door in the winter to keep out the cold.

It was caught back now with what appeared to be a tough rope of the same material.

He unhitched it from the hooks, letting the curtain fall forward, and handed it to his friend.

Bending down, Charles tied the Solicitor's legs together, turned him over somewhat roughly, and, pulling a handkerchief out of his pocket, tied his wrists behind his back.

As he did so he said with a note of laughter in his voice:

"We need yours to gag him."

"Yes, of course," Jimmy agreed obligingly.

He took his handkerchief from his pocket, then as if there was no need for them to speak of what was required, he lifted Mr. Jacobson up by the shoulders, Charles took his legs, and they carried him through the door which led into the yard.

There was nobody about because it was still teeming with rain, but still they carried the unconscious Solicitor a little way down the road from which they had approached the Inn.

"This will do," Charles said.

He and Jimmy swung the still-unconscious man backwards, forwards, and then back again, before they flung him into a deep ditch at the side of the road.

There was a splash as he fell, then without waiting to see whether or not his head was above the water, they ran quickly back into the Inn.

The girl was waiting for them, her hands clasped together almost as if she were praying, and as they came into the Lounge, shaking the rain off themselves like two dogs, she said in a voice that trembled:

"What have you . . . done with . . . him?"

"Thrown him where he will not be found for a long time. At least, not until we have all got away from here."

"Are you . . . sure?"

"Quite sure," Charles said reassuringly, "and as it has been a shock, I suggest you have a little brandy. It will make you feel better."

The girl did not refuse, and when Charles opened the door of the Parlour, she went ahead of them and sat down in a chair by the fire.

For the first time Charles looked at her, and with her red hair glinting in the firelight, her huge eyes in her very small, pointed face raised to his, he thought he must be dreaming.

Never could he have imagined that he would see anybody so attractive, so lovely, and playing a part in a drama which he had found exceedingly enjoyable.

It was almost, he thought, what he and Jimmy might have encountered when they were at Oxford, and they had both found life less exciting and much duller since they had left.

With an engaging smile which many women had found irresistible he said:

"Now suppose you tell us about yourself and why you are travelling alone, pursued by a swine like that?"

For a moment she did not answer but looked up at him a little nervously, until as if he would reassure her Charles said:

"Let me introduce myself. I am Lord Frodham, and this is my friend Sir James Overton."

"How do you do," the girl said. "I do not know how to begin to thank you or to tell you how . . . grateful I am that . . . you came to my . . . rescue."

"Perhaps you should start by telling us who you are," Charles suggested.

The way he spoke told Jimmy he was very curious.

"My name is Indira Rowlandson."

"That is a very beautiful name," Jimmy remarked.

"It is Indian, and I have just arrived from India, where I was with my father . . . until . . . on the voyage home he . . . died."

Indira gave a little sob before she went on:

"He contracted a fever of some sort, and almost before I realised how ill he was, he had died . . . and was . . . buried at . . . sea."

"I am sorry," Charles said. "But surely you have some relations you can go to?"

"That is what I meant to do," Indira said, "but Papa had written to his firm of Solicitors, saying that they were to meet us at Southampton, and . . . Mr. Jacobson was there . . . waiting."

She shivered.

"How could your father have chosen such a horrible man to handle his affairs?" Charles asked.

"It was, I believe, quite a reputable firm when the Senior Partner was in charge," Indira replied. "But he is now very old, and Mr. Jacobson told me he now runs everything."

"What happened?" Charles asked.

"Mr. Jacobson said he would look after me and there was no reason for me not to trust him. He said he was taking me to London, but when I talked about finding my relatives, he told me what he was planning."

She drew in her breath as she went on:

"He said that one of his clients, Lord Bredon, was deeply in debt and had to marry an heiress in order to save himself from going to prison."

"So you are an heiress," Jimmy interposed.

"Yes, Papa was very rich, and he left me everything he

possessed. I have the handling of it if I marry, or rather my husband will, but until then I can use only the income until I am twenty-one, and then I can control the whole fortune if I have not found anyone I want to marry."

It was, Charles thought, a sensible Will that a clever man might make, to safeguard his daughter, but Mr. Rowlandson had obviously not expected that his Solicitor would prove to be crooked.

"Do you really want to go into a Convent?" Jimmy asked.

"There is nothing . . . else I can . . . do," Indira replied. "Anything would be better than to marry a man who only wants my money and was stupid and dissolute enough to lose his own."

She spoke scathingly, but there was also, as the two men listening were aware, a touch of terror in her voice.

"I will be safe in a . . . Convent," she said as if she spoke to herself, "then I will not be . . . frightened by men, whom I . . . hate!"

She spoke spontaneously, hardly aware that she was speaking to two of the species, then added quickly:

"Oh, please . . . do not think I am being . . . rude when you have both been so kind . . . and I am very . . . grateful to you, but ever since Papa died it has been very, very . . . difficult for me. There were . . . men on the . . . ship, and then . . . Lord Bredon."

As she was so attractive, there was no need to tell Charles and Jimmy what had happened, and after a moment's silence Charles said:

"You must have some idea where your relatives are."

"My father has an aunt, but she must be very old, and I am sure there are cousins, but I never troubled to make a list of them, nor to listen at all carefully when Papa was talking about them. There were so many other things that made him so exciting to be with, and when we were in India, England seemed very far . . . away."

There was something wistful in the way she spoke. Then there was a little pause, and Charles looked at Jimmy, and they each knew what the other was thinking.

Almost as if fate had taken a hand in their affairs, Charles said:

"I can understand you wanting to go into a Convent, but I think I have a better idea, and if we have helped you, perhaps you would be kind enough to help us."

"I will if I can."

"There is a question I have to ask you first," Charles said. "First, what exactly was your father's position in life, and why did he have so much money?"

Indira hesitated. Then, as if she was thinking exactly what she should answer, she replied:

"It is rather difficult to put into words, but I suppose you could say he was a trader in many different fields."

There was a smile on Charles's face, as if this was what he had expected.

Then he said:

"And now, Miss Rowlandson, will you please listen to me?"

Chapter Two

IT IS impossible, I could not do anything like that!" Indira exclaimed.

"Why not?" Charles enquired. "You are far too pretty to go into a Convent. But if you are intent on it, there is nothing to stop you from doing it later."

Indira was obviously reflecting on what he had said, and looking so lovely as she did so that Jimmy was staring at her almost as if he felt she could not be real.

Finally she asked:

"This Marquis who says such unkind things about women . . . what is he like?"

"Tall, handsome, and irresistibly attractive to the female sex," Charles replied.

The way he spoke made Indira look at him speculatively for a moment before she said:

"He has obviously . . . hurt you . . . personally in some . . . way."

Jimmy laughed.

"That is very perceptive of you. Of course he has! He took away a very lovely—lady on whom Charles had set his heart, and that is such a familiar story in London that there is hardly a man who does not bear him a grudge in one way or another."

The way Indira looked at Jimmy as he was speaking made Charles wonder if she had noticed the perceptive pause before Jimmy had said the word "lady."

Then he told himself that the girl they were talking to was far too young to know anything about "Cyprians" and "Ladybirds."

As if he thought it was a subject to be skated over quickly, he said:

"What my friend and I are begging you to do, Miss Rowlandson, is to help us win a bet and at the same time to teach the Marquis of Ardsley a lesson. I cannot believe that you would approve of any man who is so stuck up and so very pleased with himself."

"No, of course not," Indira agreed. "In fact I hate all men, and that is a very good reason why I would like to go to a Convent."

"You will hate that," Jimmy said. "Think of being shut up for the rest of your life with a lot of women who will loathe you because you are much prettier than they are."

Indira's eyes widened and she looked at him in a startled fashion.

"Do you think that is true?" she asked. "I thought Nuns were too dedicated to God to feel jealous or envious of other women."

Charles laughed.

"If you ask me, however many prayers she may utter, a woman will still be a woman, and quite frankly, Miss Rowlandson, you are far too beautiful to be a Nun."

"Then what . . . can I . . . do?" Indira asked helplessly.

"Do what we suggest!" Charles said. "We promise you we will protect you, and we will certainly stop anybody like that ghastly Solicitor from forcing you into a marriage with a fortune-hunter."

He paused before he said:

"When our little adventure is over, which is what it will be, and you have confounded the Marquis, I promise you I will find you somewhere to go."

He realised as he spoke that Jimmy was looking at him questioningly, and he added:

"I have a mass of relations, and so have you, Jimmy, who would be only too pleased to chaperone Miss Rowlandson or to travel with her."

The two young men looked at each other and they each knew the other was thinking that because she was very rich as well as beautiful, the world was at Indira Rowlandson's feet.

It was certainly true that both of them could find relations who would be more than willing to undertake the task of looking after such an attractive girl and to introduce her to Society, in which she would undoubtedly shine.

It was obviously impossible for her to enter the *Beaw Monde* as the daughter of a tradesman, but there were a great number of people who were not so particular, especially in the country.

Both Charles and Jimmy were already mentally making a list of their poorer relations who they were quite certain would be interested in such a proposition.

Almost as if Indira knew what they were thinking, she looked from one to the other before she said:

"It is very ... kind of you ... but of course ... when I have time I am sure I can find some of Papa's ... relatives."

She made an exasperated little sound before she said:

"How could I have been so foolish as not to listen to Papa when he was telling me what we would do when we reached England? But I was thinking of the big house that he intended to rent in London, and the horses he wanted to race at Newmarket and Epsom, and I was not particularly interested in who would be with us, as I so much liked being along with him."

As she said the last words there was a note in her voice as if she wanted to cry at losing him, and Charles said hastily:

"I am quite certain your father would not want you to do anything so foolish as to incarcerate yourself in a Convent just because you are alone and have been upset by the behaviour of that swine Jacobson."

"That reminds me," Jimmy said. "It would be wise to leave here as soon as we can. When he regains consciousness he might somehow manage to get back here and make a scene."

Indira gave a little cry and started to her feet.

"You are quite right! I must get away at once! Please, do not let us stay here a moment . . . longer than we . . . have to!"

While they had been talking, the storm had passed and the rain had ceased.

Charles looked out the window, then at Indira. With her red hair streaming over her shoulders she certainly looked very lovely.

At the same time, he thought he could hardly arrive to stay with the Marquis with a woman who was dressed as a Nun.

"Have you any other clothes with you?" he asked.

"Yes, of course," Indira replied. "There are three trunks and a bonnet-box in the carriage that I hired to bring me here. I think it was because they are heavy that Mr. Jacobson was able to catch up with me."

Jimmy walked towards the door.

"I will have them sent upstairs," he said, "and I suggest you change as quickly as possible. Charles will tell you what to wear."

Jimmy went from the small Parlour, and Charles said to Indira almost as if he were talking to a child:

"Now what we must do is to concoct some tale to explain why we are bringing you to Ardsley Hall. I think perhaps it would be easiest to say we had to rescue you from High-waymen."

Indira laughed.

"That sounds very exciting!"

"Only in retrospect," Charles said. "When it happens, it is exceedingly unpleasant, as I know to my cost."

"You have been held up by Highwaymen?"

"Yes, but I will tell you about it another time," Charles answered. "Now listen to me carefully."

"I am listening."

She raised her eyes to his as she spoke, and Charles thought she had not only beautiful eyes but very strange ones.

They had a sort of mystery about them that he had never seen before, and he told himself with satisfaction that the Marquis was going to find her very intriguing.

Then, as he realised that Indira was waiting for him to speak, he began:

"You are a Lady of Quality who has just arrived in this country from India. It is always wise to keep as near to the truth as possible. You were chaperoned on the voyage by some extremely respectable people."

He paused and said quietly:

"Jimmy and I will think of names for them later. And when you arrived at Southampton, to your surprise there was nobody to meet you."

"Our Mr. Jacobson!" Indira murmured, but Charles continued as if she had not spoken:

"You therefore very bravely hired a carriage to take you to London, only to be held up by Highwaymen who fought with the Coachmen, leaving them too bruised and battered to take you any farther, and stole your horses."

Indira laughed.

"That is certainly dramatic, and just like a story in a book."

"I am rather pleased with it myself," Charles admitted. "That is how we found you, and as we did not like to disappoint our friend the Marquis by not turning up as he expected, we decided that rather than escort you to London, we would bring you to stay with him."

Indira clapped her hands together.

"That is a marvellous tale!"

"What is?" Jimmy asked, coming in through the door.

Charles quickly repeated what he had just said to Indira.

"Good gracious!" Jimmy exclaimed. "You will be writing a book if you are not careful."

"I might consider that," Charles said loftily. "In the meantime, that is what happened, and we must all tell the same story."

"Yes, of course," Jimmy agreed.

"I will go change," Indira said.

They both realised that she was nervous in case Mr. Jacobson reappeared.

"Yes, hurry!" Charles exclaimed. "Jimmy and I will try to think of a grand title for you, because do not forget that your pedigree must be impeccable. Moreover, it must not be one he might suspect to be a fraud, and therefore check it for authenticity."

As he spoke Charles looked worried.

He was astute enough to realise that this was the weak link in his and Jimmy's story.

As the Marquis was so knowledgeable about the genealogy of the people he knew, it would be dangerous to invent a title, and perhaps even more dangerous to pretend to a relationship which could not be substantiated.

While he was thinking, Indira was already moving towards the door through which Jimmy had just entered.

As he held it open for her he said:

"You will find your trunk being taken to the best bedroom, which is just at the top of the staircase."

"Thank you," she said with a smile.

"Wear the smartest travelling-clothes you possess," Charles said.

She turned her head to smile at him, then stopped.

"I have a suggestion."

"What is it?"

"If you are really going to make me out to be so important, I think it would be difficult for the Marquis to suspect I am not the daughter of the Earl of Farncombe."

"Who is he?" Charles asked.

"The Governor of Madras. Papa and I knew him in India."

"Farncombe!" Jimmy exclaimed. "If he is an Earl, then I am quite certain that the Marquis will have heard of him."

"But this Marquis has not been to India?" Indira asked.

"If he has, I am sure that we would know about it," Charles replied.

"Yes, I am sure we would," Jimmy agreed. "We would doubtless have had a lecture too on how the Indian women under the skin are just the same as the European variety."

The two men laughed, and Indira went on:

"The Earl of Farncombe in fact has a daughter just about my age. Her name is Lady Mary Combe. Even if some of the Marquis's friends have been to India, they would never have met her because she has been very ill for the last two years and has been living in the hills, where it is cooler, and only very close personal friends have been allowed to visit her."

Charles looked at Jimmy.

"It sounds a perfect alias," he said. "Thank you, Indira. That is very helpful."

"The Earl has also lived in India for many years without coming home," Indira said, "so it is very unlikely that your Marquis will have met him."

She did not wait for Charles and Jimmy to reply, but ran across the Lounge and up the oak staircase at the end of it.

Jimmy shut the door behind her.

"Fate has certainly taken a hand in our affairs," he said. "I never dreamt that we would be lucky enough to find anybody so attractive and exactly what we need."

"I listened very carefully," Charles said, "and she never mispronounced a word in a manner which might have given her away as being a tradesman's daughter."

"She has obviously been very well educated," Jimmy said. "But of course no real Lady would have travelled alone."

"How could she help it when her father died?"

"I do not know, but I expect the Captain would have found her a Chaperone or someone like that."

The two men were silent until Jimmy said:

"When we have confounded the Marquis with her, we will have to look after her and see that that swine Jacobson does not harass her again."

"I have met Bredon," Charles said reflectively.

"You have?" Jimmy exclaimed. "What is he like?"

"Ghastly! He got sacked from Eton, and when he came into the title after his father's death, he gambled away every penny he possessed in two years."

"No wonder he has been looking for an heiress," Jimmy remarked.

"The only thing he has left to sell is his title," Charles said, "and when I last saw him at some Dance-Hall about six months ago, he looked dissipated and down-at-heel. He was also very unpleasantly drunk."

"Well, we have saved the pretty redhead from him for the moment."

"Pretty?" Charles exclaimed. "She is lovely! And I am sure we can find her a decent husband who would be kind to her."

"I am even prepared to be kind to her myself," Jimmy said, "but I think my family would shoot me if I married a tradesman's daughter."

"So would mine," Charles agreed.

"Well, I am quite certain that at the suggestion of any other position in our lives, she would be off to the Convent again."

"I am sure she would," Jimmy said. "At the same time, it is the greatest bit of luck that she dislikes men. It means she will keep the Marquis at arm's length, and that will surprise him. Apart from anything else, he is quite certain he is irresistible."

"He is," Charles said drily. "We established that a long time ago."

He spoke so bitterly that Jimmy decided to change the subject.

"One thing I will say is that our lady-friend is exceedingly sporting. Most women do not have the guts, as you and I well know, to run away on their own from a blackguard Solicitor, or to agree to the extraordinary proposition we have put to her."

"She is exceptional," Charles agreed. "I am only rather nervous in case the Marquis penetrates her impersonation the moment he sees her."

Jimmy gave a cry of horror.

"Now you are inviting disaster! If you are afraid he may be suspicious, then perhaps he will read your thoughts, or if you are obviously on edge he may suspect that something is up."

"You are right," Charles conceded. "I remember one of those old bores at the Club who was always droning on about how he rescued people during the French Revolution saying: 'The art of disguise is to think oneself into the part'!"

"Exactly! And we have to believe absolutely in the tale we tell the Marquis, and make sure Indira Rowlandson does the same."

"The same what?" a voice asked, and as the two gentlemen rose to their feet Indira came into the Parlour.

She was looking very different from when she had left them, and for a moment both Charles and Jimmy stared at her, speechless with admiration.

She was wearing an exceedingly smart travelling-coat of sapphire-blue satin edged with braid which made a pattern round the hem and round the sleeves.

Her bonnet, which was in the very latest fashion, had a high, pointed brim which was edged with a row of lace, and the high crown was decorated with tightly curled ostrich-feathers of the same blue as her coat.

Her shoes, gloves, and bag all matched, and it flashed through Charles's mind that they were in fact being deceived and to be so smartly dressed she must have come straight from London.

As if she understood his astonishment and could read his thoughts, Indira said:

"You look surprised, but Papa's organisation is so splendid that my clothes were made in Paris and sent out to India, or wherever we were, every six months."

"You look magnificent," Charles said, recovering his voice, "and exactly as we wish you to look."

"Thank you, My Lord, but now let us be on our way. I am so afraid that Mr. Jacobson will reappear and I will have to start running away all over again."

"You are not running anywhere except with us," Jimmy said firmly. "I will see to your trunks being put on the Phaeton, or perhaps we will be able to hire some sort of vehicle to follow us."

"Oh, please," Indira said quickly, "if possible let us take my trunks with us. Now that Papa is dead, I feel they are the only things I possess, and I am so afraid of losing them."

"Yes, of course," Charles said soothingly. "I understand exactly what you are feeling."

He paused before he said:

"I do not want to seem inquisitive, but will you be able to get hold of any of your money without having to contact that reptile who has behaved so badly towards you?"

"Oh, yes," Indira answered. "I can go to Papa's Bank in London and I am sure when I identify myself they will let me draw on his account. I know too that they hold some securities which are in my name."

Charles looked at her in admiration, thinking that few young women would be so knowledgeable or so sensible about their finances.

Then he thought that as a tradesman's daughter she would understand the handling of money, while a débutante in the Social World would never have to bother her pretty head with such mundane matters.

There was no time for any more conversation, for Jimmy came hurrying back to say that the trunks were being strapped on the back of the Phaeton, and although it meant their groom would have to hold Indira's hat-box on his knees, they could take everything.

"Let us go at once!" Charles said. "It is a good thing you are slim, Miss Rowlandson, because three is always a squeeze in a Phaeton which is made for two."

"I would put up with anything to get away from here and be quite certain that Mr. Jacobson will not be able to find me."

"I doubt if he will be in a position to find anybody for the next twenty-four hours," Jimmy said. "Of course, there is also a chance that he may have drowned in the ditch, in which case you will not have to worry about him ever again."

"I suppose it is wicked of me to say so, but that would give me a great deal of . . . pleasure."

"Wicked or not, I feel the same," Charles added.

She laughed.

They drove out of the courtyard of the Inn, with the Landlord bowing them good-bye, having been handsomely reimbursed for his hospitality.

Only when they had driven on for a short while did Jimmy say:

"Forgive me for asking you, but what did you do with the Nun's robe you were wearing? It would be a mistake for the maids who will unpack for you at Ardsley Hall to discover it."

"I thought of that," Indira replied, "and because I was aware it might be incriminating evidence if Mr. Jacobson was searching for me, I stuffed it up the chimney."

Charles and Jimmy both burst into laughter.

"You are magnificent!" Charles said when he could speak. "And I am quite certain I shall win my bet."

"I am feeling somewhat apprehensive that you may," Jimmy replied, "but you have a long way to go yet."

"Now, tell me more about the Marquis," Indira said. "Supposing after all the trouble you have taken in introducing me into the house, he takes no further interest in me, and . . ."

"He will take an interest in you," Jimmy interrupted. "You are the most beautiful girl I have ever seen, and I think I know every beauty in London by this time. I know Charles will say the same."

"Beauty means different things to different people," Charles remarked, "but if the Marquis is not bowled over by Miss Rowlandson, then I am a blind man."

There was a little pause. Then Indira asked:

"What do you . . . mean, 'bowled over'? You are not . . . expecting that he will fall . . . in love with . . . me?"

The way she spoke made Charles and Jimmy aware that she thought it so horrifying that she might now, at the very last moment, refuse to go on with the act.

"No, no, of course not," Charles said soothingly. "Ardsley has never been in love with anybody. You can be quite certain about that. We just want to make sure that he finds you extremely attractive and believes you to be *crème de la crème,* which is what, with his infallible instinct, he expects in a woman to whom he offers his friendship."

Charles emphasised the word "friendship" to reassure Indira, but as Jimmy knew she was still anxious he said:

"Because he will believe you to be a Lady of Quality and unmarried, I assure you he would not try to kiss you, or anything like that."

Indira gave a little cry of horror.

"Are you sure . . . quite sure? If he did, I should have to . . . run away again, and . . . nothing you could say would . . . persuade me to . . . stay."

"I promise you will be quite safe," Jimmy said, "but it will certainly surprise him if you do not wish to flirt with him."

"Flirt with him!" Indira exclaimed. "I have no wish to flirt with anybody! The men on the ship . . . after Papa was . . . dead would . . . never leave me . . . alone."

Because she was sitting between Charles and Jimmy and they were so close together, they were both aware of the shudder that ran through her body as she remembered what had happened.

"Then," she went on, "when Mr. Jacobson told me I was to marry a man I had never seen, and would not listen when I told him I would rather die than do so, I was frightened, very, very . . . frightened that somehow he would . . . force me to . . . obey . . . him."

"That is what he might have done," Charles said, "and that is why you must be very careful not to encourage the Marquis or any other man in the house-party."

"What do you mean—encourage?"

"Be polite, somewhat aloof, and do not laugh too loudly or too frequently at what they are saying, and . . ."

He paused, then said:

"Oh, go on, Jimmy, you can explain better than I can."

"What Charles is trying to say," Jimmy began, "is that real Ladies of Quality, like this daughter of the Earl you are pretending to be, would be somewhat reserved and would not encourage a man to pay her compliments. If he did, she would seem shy and a little bashful."

"In which case," Indira said in a low voice, "he would not . . . force himself upon . . . me?"

"Not if he was a gentleman," Charles said sharply, "and certainly not if we are about. What you have to do, Miss Rowlandson, is to think of us as if we were your brothers."

Indira gave a little sigh.

"I always wished I had a brother, and Papa was very, very disappointed when I was not a boy."

"Well, you have two brothers now," Jimmy said. "Charles and I will look after you and see that no-one insults you in any way or does anything you do not like! You can be quite certain of one thing: we will keep away any brutes like Jacobson or fortune-hunters like Bredon."

"Of course," Charles agreed, "and there is something else you must remember: you are not rich, and you rely entirely on your father for any money you have. He is generous, but you own nothing personally."

"I understand," Indira said.

Charles thought that her father had trained her well and felt quite certain that a Society Girl would have asked innumerable questions on this particular score alone.

"I will tell you another thing we have to think of," Jimmy said. "Where was Lady Mary supposed to be going when she hired the carriage at Southampton?"

"I have thought of that already," Charles replied. "About ten miles away from here I have two very boring old cousins. They never do anything or go anywhere. I know they are both alive because my mother had a letter from them about ten days ago."

"So Lady Mary was going to stay with them!" Jimmy interposed.

"Exactly!" Charles agreed. "They were friends of her father's, and actually I believe my cousin Harold was in India about a century ago."

"You do not suppose the Marquis knows them?"

"I am quite certain if he has ever heard of them he would make every effort to avoid them," Charles said. "I have told you, they are bores, and no-one in their right mind would want to entertain them, although they are highly respectable."

"What is their name?" Indira asked.

"Colonel and Mrs. Toddington," Charles answered, "and I will tell the Marquis that I have sent a message to them to say that you will not be arriving until we can escort you there safely after the Steeple-Chase is over."

"Really, Charles, you are a genius at improvisation!"

Jimmy exclaimed. "I had no idea you had such imagination! There is almost a magical quality about it!"

"I think he is very clever," Indira said. "And now that I know the whole story of my background, I think also that as I have been through such an unpleasant experience with the Highwaymen, I would not want to talk about it."

"That is sensible," Charles approved. "I have always been told that one lie leads to another, and the less you say, the less you will become involved."

"It is certainly an . . . adventure that I did not expect," Indira said in a small voice, "and since I am with you I find I am not really as frightened about meeting the Marquis as I was at the thought of . . . begging the Convent to take me in."

"How did you know about the Convent in the first place?" Charles asked, curious.

"There was a Nun on board ship who was very kind to me after Papa died. She nursed him when he had the fever."

"So she told you about it?"

"Yes, she said if ever I was in trouble I was to go there and mention her name, and they would look after me."

"The Convent is not the right place for you," Charles said firmly.

"I am beginning to think that myself," Indira agreed. "But when Mr. Jacobson met me when I came off the boat and took me to an Hotel, and told me what he had planned for me, I was absolutely frantic."

"So you got hold of a Nun's habit in which to escape from him."

"I thought he would not be looking for me dressed as a Nun," Indira said simply. "So I bribed the chambermaid to buy me a Nun's robe."

"How on earth did she know where to buy one?" Jimmy enquired.

"She was very clever about that," Indira answered. "She

was sure there would not be one in the shops, so she offered one of the Little Sisters of the Poor, who work in the slums round the dockyard at Southampton, five pounds for her robe. I presume she had two, and the money was tempting."

"I can see you are a born adventuress," Charles said, "and not only brave but undefeatable."

"I hope so," Indira replied, "but I am very . . . afraid of the . . . future without Papa to . . . look after me."

As there was nothing they could say to this, they drove on in silence.

It was Indira who broke it by saying:

"You may think it . . . foolish of me, but I am so nervous that I may forget my own name or not answer when I am addressed as Mary."

Jimmy turned his head to look at her and Charles was listening as she went on:

"Would it be possible when you got to know me . . . better to call me Indira? We could say I was Christened 'Mary Indira.'"

Jimmy did not answer for a moment and she said hastily:

"Not if you think it would be a mistake. But it would make me feel I was still . . . close to . . . Papa."

"Of course you can be Indira to us," Charles said, "and I think it's a charming and original name."

"Thank you . . . thank you!" Indira cried, and gave him such a beguiling smile that Jimmy thought no-one could be lovelier.

They drove for another half-an-hour and the light was fading when Charles exclaimed:

"There it is—that is Ardsley Hall!"

There was a gap in the trees which bordered the road, and through it on a high rise Indira could see a magnificent building of grey stone.

It was certainly architecturally attractive, and at the same time it was large enough to house a Regiment.

The Marquis's standard was high above the roof-tops,

and as they turned in at the imposing wrought-iron gates with lodges on either side constructed to look like small Castles, Jimmy thought that no girl who had just come from abroad could fail to be impressed.

Indira did not say anything, but he was aware that she was tense, and as they reached the end of the drive and the house seemed to loom above them, vast and somehow menacing, he felt that Charles was tense too.

A large dome rose above the centre of the building and commodious wings extended on each side. A great flight of grey stone steps led up to the front door, and as Charles brought his horses to a standstill, grooms came running to their heads.

A red carpet was run down the stone steps up which they were to walk.

"Keep your chin high," Jimmy said in a whisper to Indira as they reached an enormous Hall where there were a great number of footmen wearing powdered wigs, white knee-breeches, and a resplendent livery in the Ardsley colours,

A white-haired Butler bowed to Charles.

"Lord Frodham, I believe. His Lordship is expecting you and your—party."

It was obvious from the way the Butler spoke that his eyes rested on Indira with a slight expression of surprise.

He went ahead of them with pompous dignity, and only when he reached a pair of mahogany doors did he pause to ask:

"May I have the names of your friends, M'Lord?"

"Lady Mary Combe and Sir James Overton."

The Butler opened the door and announced them in a voice that seemed to ring out round the large room and reach the four people at the other end of it.

The Marquis came towards them, and as he did so Charles thought however infuriating he might be, there was no doubt that their host was an extremely handsome man and had, when he chose to use it, an undeniable charm.

"How nice to see you, Frodham," he said, holding out his hand. "I was growing worried that you might have had an unpleasant journey owing to the thunderstorm."

"It certainly delayed us," Charles admitted, "but there is another reason why we are later than we intended."

The Marquis was already holding out his hand to Jimmy, saying:

"It is a pleasure to see you, Overton!"

And now he was looking at Indira questioningly.

"May I introduce the Marquis of Ardsley?" Charles asked her, then said to the Marquis, "This is Lady Mary Combe, whom Jimmy and I have just rescued from an appalling experience with some Highwaymen who not only stole her money but also her horses."

"Highwaymen!" the Marquis exclaimed. "What a terrible thing to happen!"

Indira gave him a little curtsey and put her hand in his. The Marquis, holding it firmly, was aware as he did so that her fingers trembled.

"You are suffering from shock," he said, "and it is not surprising. Come and sit down. Let me bring you a glass of champagne."

"Thank you," Indira murmured. "It was . . . very frightening."

Without relinquishing her hand, the Marquis drew her towards the fireplace, where he introduced her to his other guests—two men and a lady—all of whom exclaimed in horror and consternation at what she must have been through.

"The Highwaymen are becoming a perfect pest on the roads!" said one of the gentlemen, whose name she had not heard. "Something ought to be done about them, and I intend to raise the question in the House of Commons."

"I wish you would do that, Edmund," the Marquis said. "What we need is a local Police Force to keep a watch on the main highways. As it is, when they are sent for the Military always arrive too late."

"That is true," Jimmy said. "My father always complained that in our County it is impossible to catch a Highwayman, who has in every case several hours' start of his pursuers."

The Marquis had fetched a glass of champagne, which he handed to Indira before he offered any to Charles and Jimmy.

Then he sat down beside her on the sofa and said:

"I am sure you do not want to talk about your experience, and because I know how frightening it must have been, I suggest we talk of other things. Let me say first how delighted I am to be able to offer you my hospitality tonight. I hope that wherever you are going we can persuade you to stay and watch the Steeple-Chase."

"That is very . . . kind of . . . you," Indira said in a small voice.

Charles turned to Indira.

"I told you we were right to bring you here and that His Lordship would welcome you."

Indira smiled in a manner which he thought looked shy and reserved, and he explained to the Marquis:

"At first Jimmy and I thought we should take her on to where she was going. But it is at least fifteen miles in the opposite direction, and there was every likelihood of it starting to rain again, so we thought it best to come straight here."

"I think it very sensible of you," the Marquis approved, "but surely Lady Mary was not travelling alone?"

"I was unaccompanied after a long chapter of accidents," Indira said before Charles could reply. "I have just . . . arrived from . . . India."

"From India!" the Marquis exclaimed.

"Yes. My father . . . died . . . on the voyage."

There was a little pause before she went on:

"We were supposed to be met by a Courier and, I believed, several relatives, but when the ship docked there was nobody!"

"Blame the post!" Jimmy exclaimed. "It is getting ridiculous how bad the overseas mail is, despite the fact that the Government boasts about its efficiency."

"I agree with you," one of the Marquis's other guests affirmed. "My father is in Egypt at the moment, and I have not heard one single word from him since he left, although he always writes to me at least twice a week."

"It is a scandal," the Marquis agreed. "But tell us, Lady Mary, what happened."

"I thought the best thing I could do would be to hire a carriage and drive to the house of my father's friends, where I was to stay. I had quite a pleasant journey until . . . the Highwaymen . . . held me up."

Her voice faltered, and both Charles and Jimmy thought she was acting her part admirably.

"You must have been very frightened," the Marquis's lady guest replied. "I know I should have fallen into a swoon, or screamed for help."

"There was no point in my doing either of those things," Indira said, "because I was in an empty lane, and although the Coachman and the footman on the box tried to defend me, the Highwaymen knocked them to the ground, then stole the horses. That was what they were really interested in."

"But they took your money too."

"Fortunately, I did not carry a large amount in my bag, and because Lord Frodham and Sir James appeared, the Highwaymen did not have time to rifle my trunks."

"You poor, poor thing!" the lady exclaimed. "My heart bleeds for you. How lucky that these two charming gentlemen came to help you."

"I am very . . . very . . . grateful to them for . . . saving me, and driving the men away, who were very . . . frightening," Indira said.

"I am sure what you would like to do now," the lady suggested, "is to have a little rest before dinner. Shall I take her upstairs, Seldon?"

"Yes, of course, Rosie," he replied.

As he spoke her Christian name, Charles and Jimmy gave each other a knowing look.

As Charles had said in White's, Lady Sinclair, who was described as a "Rose of England," had captured the attention of the elusive, fastidious, and at the same time discriminating Marquis of Ardsley.

Now both young men were thinking to themselves somewhat dismally that because Lady Sinclair was at Ardsley Hall, it was unlikely that the Marquis would be "bowled over," as they had put it, by their protégée.

At the same time, there was no doubt that Indira was the more spectacular of the two.

Lady Sinclair, while very lovely in the conventional English pink, white, and gold manner, paled a little, in their estimation at any rate, in comparison with Indira's flaming red hair.

Her white skin, which they had not appreciated until now, was, in the light of the candles that had been lit in the Salon, like the petals of a magnolia.

"Thank you very much," Indira was saying to Lady Sinclair. "I would like to go upstairs and, as you suggest . . . lie down."

She rose to her feet before she said to the Marquis:

"It is very kind of you, My Lord, to have me here as an unexpected and uninvited guest. I hope I shall not prove a bother for tonight, and I think perhaps it would be . . . best if I would . . . leave tomorrow."

"I am quite certain," the Marquis replied, "that we can persuade you to stay and watch your two rescuers, Lord

Frodham and Sir James, competing in my Steeple-Chase. They are very experienced riders, and I may tell you they are up against some stiff competition."

"Especially where it concerns our host," Charles added. "We were thinking, My Lord, that it would be a sporting gesture, since you have the best horses and know the course better than we do, if you were severely handicapped."

"It is an idea, but it is certainly one I would not agree to with any enthusiasm," the Marquis said.

"I was afraid of that," Charles replied, "in which case, Lady Mary, you will see your host receive the Steeple-Chase Cup which he himself has provided and which, however hard we compete for it and for how ever many years, is likely to remain at Ardsley Hall."

Everybody laughed, and the Marquis threw up his hands in dismay.

"What can I say but suggest that we abandon the whole idea of a Steeple-Chase and instead make it merely a Show with a prize for the most beautiful woman on horseback."

As the Marquis spoke, Charles noticed that Lady Sinclair gave a self-conscious little laugh, as if she was quite certain who would win the prize.

At the same time, he did not miss the fact that the Marquis was looking at Indira, and her eyes in the light of the candles seemed even more mysterious than they had in the Parlour when he had first noticed them.

Too, he had the feeling that as Lady Sinclair linked her arm with Indira's and drew her towards the door, she was glad to take her out of the Marquis's orbit.

'So far, so good!' he thought to himself, and knew that Jimmy was thinking the same.

*

As they walked up the stairs, Lady Sinclair said to Indira:

"You must be feeling very shaken and distressed. I am sure if you would rather retire to bed and have a light meal sent up to your room, our host would understand. Everything in this house is done to make the guests feel happy and at home, and perhaps after your traumatic experience it would be wiser to take things very easy."

"Thank you for your concern," Indira replied, "but perhaps after I have rested I shall be able to decide what is best for me to do."

"That is very sensible," Lady Sinclair agreed, "but you must not take any risks with yourself. Shock often has a delayed action, as I know to my own cost."

She went into a rather incoherent tale of what had happened after she had once had a shock from being involved in a fire.

When she had finished it they had reached the room where Indira was to be sleeping and where two maids were already unpacking her trunk.

"I will leave you now," Lady Sinclair said, "and do not hesitate to stay in bed, if you feel it is an effort to rise again."

"Thank you for being so kind," Indira replied.

However, she was astute enough to realise that Lady Sinclair's kindness was not entirely concern for her health.

As the maids unpacked her things, she thought with satisfaction that her gowns, which came from Paris, would certainly not look out-of-place at Ardsley Hall, magnificent though it was.

The maids helped her to undress and she got into bed, and when they had left her and she was alone, she lay thinking of how lucky it was that she had been able to escape, with the help of Lord Frodham and Sir James, from that horrible Mr. Jacobson.

"How could I have known that he was a crook?" she asked herself. "If Papa were alive he would be furious at his behaviour!"

She had been so close to her father and he had discussed so many things with her that she thought that the wise thing for her to do would be to go to Coutt's Bank and explain to the Manager what had happened.

She would ask him to find her a new firm of Solicitors who would take over her business affairs, and whom the Bank would vouch for as being both reliable and honest.

Even as she reasoned it out calmly, she found herself afraid of being without her father, who had meant everything in her life since her mother had died.

She had loved him and he had loved her, and because they were constantly travelling about, she had been truthful when she told Charles and Jimmy that she was not certain how she could find her relations in England or indeed who they were.

It was over ten years since she had last been in her own country, and as she had been only eight years old at the time, she could hardly remember anything about it.

Her father's interests were in the East, and while England was at war with France, he had thought it not only a waste of time but dangerous to attempt the long sea-voyage home.

But because her father was determined that she should be properly educated, her Governesses and Tutors travelled with them as they moved from one Eastern country to another.

Because he was so rich and of such importance in his own world, a large entourage of those he employed always accompanied them.

Since they were never intrusive when her father wished to be alone with her and she with him, it was quite easy to forget the company of paid employees whose special charge they were.

Now suddenly her father had died and she was completely alone.

Because the majority of those they had employed over the years were foreigners, they had set out to return to England with only a lady's-maid for herself and a secretary and a valet for her father.

The former had succumbed to the same fever as had killed him, and the valet, whom Indira had never particularly liked, had left at Cape Town.

Her lady's-maid was French, and when the ship stopped at Marseilles she had begged Indira that she might go to Paris and see her mother before she rejoined her in London.

Indira was perceptive enough to realise that once she had arrived home she would never see the woman again.

She did not think it would matter much, being sure that it would be a mistake after the long years of war for her to arrive in England with a French servant.

She had thought there would be the usual crowd of attendants waiting for her at Southampton, and she knew that her father had instructed his Solicitors to arrange everything for their convenience.

It was therefore a shock and a very unpleasant one when there was only Mr. Jacobson, who abruptly and rudely told her she was to be married to Lord Bredon, so that she could come into her father's money three years before she would possess it otherwise.

At first she could hardly believe she had to listen to such an outrageous idea, but when he became unpleasantly threatening, she told him she wished to retire to her bedroom, feeling exhausted after her father's death and the long voyage.

Mr. Jacobson had agreed, and when she was alone, Indira had made up her mind to escape.

She fortunately had a lot of money with her because her father never travelled without considerable sums of ready cash.

The difficulty was, what could she do?

It was then that she thought with horror of the trouble she had had on the voyage when she was alone without her father's protection, when men of all ages pursued her relentlessly, and whether it was because of her looks or her money was immaterial.

She then decided that the only possible way she could escape them and Mr. Jacobson was to go into a Convent.

With the same efficiency that had characterised her father's dealings, she had put her plan into operation.

She was relieved when she drove away from the Hotel at dawn the next morning before Mr. Jacobson could make enquiries as to what time she would be ready to leave with him for London.

It was only because the carriage provided for her was not of the quality that she was sure would have been obtained by her father that she did not get as far on her journey as she had hoped.

In another hour-and-a-half, she reckoned, she would have reached the Convent the Nun had told her about, but Mr. Jacobson had appeared, and she had been rescued only at what seemed to her to be the very last moment.

Now by some strange quirk of fate for which she was very grateful, she was lying in an extremely comfortable bed in a magnificent room with a painted ceiling in the type of house that her father had often described to her as being very much a part of England.

"If only Papa were here," Indira said to herself. "It would be so exciting to see it all with him, and hear him tell me about these people. He would not be as much impressed with them as they are with themselves!"

She knew as soon as she had met the Marquis that the way Lord Frodham and Sir James had described him was very true, if a little unkind.

He was very conscious of his own consequence, and she compared him with the men she had seen in India who governed it with pomp and circumstance besides a pride which made the Indians very conscious that they must bow to their conquerors.

"At least it will be interesting to stay here for a day or so,"

Indira told herself, "and it will give me time to think of what I can do and where I can go."

She was aware that Lord Frodham was prepared to make plans for her future, but she was not certain if she wanted a future which depended on the kindness or the patronage of any man.

"I want to be independent of them all," she said aloud.

She thought that however kind Charles and Jimmy might seem, they were still men, and she unfortunately was a woman.

Chapter Three

As THE ladies left the Dining-Room, Indira was aware that Lady Sinclair was regarding her with undisguised hostility.

Before dinner the Marquis had introduced other members of the house-party who had arrived, then said:

"I think I must honour our unexpected guest tonight, to assure her not only how delighted we are to have her here at Ardsley Hall, but also to apologise for the unpleasant treatment she received on her arrival in England, instead of the welcome she might have expected."

The story of Indira's treatment at the hands of Highwaymen had lost nothing in the telling.

One after another the guests had come up to her before dinner to say how intolerable the situation had become in the country, and that theft, robbery, and violence were becoming so habitual that something would have to be done about it.

"Of course," one Peer said, "if these felons are caught they are hanged, but that is no deterrent to a man who finds it impossible to get employment of any sort and must either starve or steal."

The argument grew quite heated and naturally the Government was blamed for being weak in providing proper protection for its citizens, and worst of all for pursuing a policy of low wages and the import of foreign goods.

Indira listened to everything that was said, and Charles and Jimmy thought approvingly that she was acting the part they required of her with an expertise that could not be equalled.

To begin with, not only did she look lovely, but her gown was obviously the envy of the lady guests, outshining theirs beyond dispute and making them, Charles thought with satisfaction, look quite dowdy in comparison.

He was knowledgeable enough about women to be aware that Indira had a grace that was unusual, which together with her red hair and white skin would have made her outstanding in any company, however many other beauties were present.

He thought she had certainly listened to him and Jimmy attentively when they had told her to seem quiet, reserved, modest, and a little shy.

Charles thought with a slight smile that, like himself, every man in the room was only too ready to protect her from Highwaymen or anything else that menaced her.

It was certainly a satisfaction to the two friends when the Marquis seated Indira on his right with Lady Sinclair on his left.

They were aware that the spoilt beauty was infuriated at taking second-place and equally aware that the Marquis, intent as usual on doing what he wished, was not in the least perturbed by her pouting red lips and the flounce with which she went into the Dining-Room on the arm of another man.

Indira was actually very hungry because she had been too frightened to linger at the Posting-Inn where her Coachman had changed horses.

She had therefore eaten only a little bread and cheese and drunk a glass of cider before she was ready to proceed on her journey and put as many miles as possible between herself and Mr. Jacobson.

She was quite certain that he would not let her get away easily, but she thought he would have no idea that her destination was a Convent.

It was only after she had driven for some hours that she had realised with dismay that she had been obliged to tell the Posting-Inn at Southampton where she was going and that when Mr. Jacobson made enquiries he would get the information he required.

She therefore sat tense in the back of the carriage, willing the horses to go faster and still faster, knowing that the animals were of inferior breeding and that the last two had been too old to travel more quickly than what she considered to be a "snail's pace."

But she had been saved, and now she thought she could never be sufficiently grateful to Charles and Jimmy.

Because they seemed to her to be young and light-hearted, she was trying to think of them as if they were in reality her brothers, and not the men she hated, who without the protection of her father made her desperately afraid both physically and mentally.

She was afraid physically because they obviously considered her beautiful, and on the ship she had been terrified that by some unscrupulous means of their own men would intrude on her in her cabin either in the daytime or at night.

After her father's death, she had ensured her safety at night by insisting that her lady's-maid sleep in her father's cabin, which communicated with her own.

Even then, she left the door open between them and instructed the woman at the slightest disturbance to run for the ship's officer who was on duty.

Fortunately, there had been no need for such dramatics. At the same time, Indira would lie awake shuddering at every footstep she heard, and feeling that even in the dark she could see men's eyes desiring her.

It was only when her father was no longer with her that she realised how protective he had been all her life and that his company of secretaries, couriers, and valets, wherever they had travelled, had all contributed to the wall of security she had always felt round her and yet had taken as a matter of course.

Now that it was no longer there, she told herself, she had to become self-sufficient.

Mentally she was too astute and too intuitive not to realise the difficulties, and it was only when Mr. Jacobson struck real terror into her that she knew that only her quick wits could save her from being married to a man she had never seen but already loathed and despised.

'I must never be in such a position again,' she thought.

She wondered if despite everything Charles and Jimmy had said it would not be better for her to enter a Convent.

She obviously could not go to the one which was now known to Mr. Jacobson, but it would not be the only Convent in England, and she was quite certain she would be accepted somewhere.

But for the moment she was safe, and as she looked down the long table at the Marquis's glittering guests, she thought it was the sort of company that her father would have wished her to be in, and it was almost as if he had had a hand in bringing her here.

"You are very quiet, Lady Mary!" the Marquis remarked beside her.

"I am sorry if I appear rude," she replied, "but I am in fact very hungry."

"Then I hope my Chef will not disappoint you."

"I am sure he will not do that. But as you say he is a Chef, can it be possible that he is French?"

"Of course he is French," the Marquis replied firmly. "No people in the world can cook as well as the French, or have such an appreciation of food."

"I have always found the Chinese cooking very good," Indira remarked.

"I have heard that," the Marquis replied, "but I cannot ever remember eating Chinese food."

"You should try it sometime. It is exciting and imaginative, and the Chinese have for generations known how to appeal to the palate because they have studied health as well as philosophy."

There was an expression of surprise in the Marquis's eyes as he said:

"Are you really interested in those subjects?"

"Of course," Indira replied, "and I hope in a great many others besides."

"Such as?"

As he spoke, the Marquis thought a little cynically that with such astounding good looks, the most obvious subject for Lady Mary would be love, and he wondered if she would be brave enough to confess it.

"I find the Eastern religions," she said in reply to his question, "fascinating and absorbing. Perhaps Buddhism is the most mystic, the most understandable of them all, and the one which draws me most."

"Why is that? Because of its belief in reincarnation?" the Marquis asked. "And who do you fancy you were in your previous life: Cleopatra, or perhaps the Queen of Sheba?"

He spoke mockingly, thinking that whenever the subject had arisen in the past, which was not very often, any woman present had always been convinced that she had been one of those exotic and enticing women.

However, Indira did not answer, and after a moment he said:

"I am waiting for your reply to my question."

"I thought we were talking seriously," she said quietly, "and as it is obviously a subject which bores Your Lordship, shall we talk of your horses, which Lord Frodham tells me are outstanding."

The way she spoke, the cold note in her voice, and the expression he saw in her eyes made the Marquis feel as if she had suddenly confronted him with a naked sword.

Never in his experience had any woman slapped him down in such a surprising manner, and certainly not anybody who looked as young and lovely and, he thought, amenable as Lady Mary.

"Forgive me," he said after he had drawn in his breath. "I was not taking you seriously for the simple reason that it is very unusual in England to find any woman of any age who knows anything about the East."

Again to his surprise, Indira did not enthuse over his apology but merely inclined her head as if she accepted it as her just due.

"Are all these gentlemen here," she asked, "taking part in your Steeple-Chase?"

"Now you are deliberately being unkind to me," the Marquis protested. "I have apologised, and quite frankly, I want to continue with our conversation about the East, and go back to when I asked you why you were drawn to Buddhism more than to the other religions you have studied."

For a moment he thought that she would refuse to answer him. Then as if she felt that politeness demanded an answer, Indira said:

"It is the only logical way of explaining the different circumstances in which we are born, and there is a justice in the Wheel of Rebirth that I cannot find in any other religion."

"You do not think the Christian attitude of promising a repentant sinner a front seat in Heaven after death if he has suffered in this world is a reasonable one?"

"No."

The Marquis waited, and when she obviously did not wish to elaborate on her reply, after a moment he said:

"I have some books in my Library which I feel sure you will find interesting. One of them, Shih Ching, was brought back to England from China many years ago by my great-great-grandfather. There is also an early edition of the *Vedas,* which I do not think can be found in any other Library in Europe."

Indira turned her head to look at him, and now there was a light in her eyes that had not been there before.

"Is that true?" she exclaimed. "How can you be so fortunate as to possess anything so unique? And please, will you allow me to see them before I leave?"

"I shall be delighted to show them to you."

"Some of the Chinese have the most magnificently illustrated manuscripts in their houses," Indira said, "but they are always very secretive about their possessions, and will only show their books, their porcelain, and their really precious drawings to somebody they think will understand the hidden meaning in them."

"They believed that you could do that?"

"I was lucky enough to be my father's daughter."

As she spoke she realised she was thinking of her real father and not the Earl of Farncombe, whom she had adopted for her pretence role.

To divert the Marquis's interest, she said quickly:

"I have always found it fascinating that every great Eastern religion always had an esoteric and secret side to it which was revealed only to the initiated. I expect you will remember reading that the ancient Egyptians, for instance, could conjure up fire by merely speaking a certain word from *The Book of the Dead*, which was read only by their specially chosen Priests."

"You are bringing back to me memories of things I have not thought about since I was at Oxford," the Marquis replied. "There, as it happens, I studied Oriental history, and I found it most intriguing."

"Then when you left Oxford you promptly forgot all about it," Indira said lightly.

"I did not forget," the Marquis contradicted, "but I placed it at the back of my mind. It was Napoleon who spoke of 'the cupboards of his mind,' and that is what I think we all do in one way or another. Although certain subjects may be shut away, you have only to open the door to rediscover them."

"I am sure that is true," Indira agreed, "but some people have very few cupboards, and some a 'Bluebeard's Chamber' where it is best to leave the door closed."

She was talking as if she were with her father, and they were exchanging points of view and arguing as if they were two Dons fencing with each other in words.

The Marquis was just about to reply when Lady Sinclair put her hand on his arm and said plaintively:

"You are neglecting me, Seldon! And it is something that has never happened to me before. I am feeling very hurt by such unkindness."

She spoke in a little-girl's voice that he had found rather intriguing when he had first met her.

Like all strong, positive men, he believed he liked women to be small, clinging, and feminine, and Lady Sinclair with her pink-and-white beauty appeared to be all that.

She was also astute enough, after a long succession of lovers, to know exactly what appealed to men.

She turned her large blue eyes up to the Marquis as if she felt the child-like appeal in them would never go unrequited, but to her surprise he merely said:

"I am sure, Rosie, that Lord Neville is only too ready to make up for my shortcomings."

As he spoke, he looked across her at her partner on her other side, a dashing Rake, the youngest son of a Duke, who was looking for a suitable heiress to keep him in the comfort in which he had been brought up and which only his eldest brother had any hope of enjoying in the future.

"If you think anybody could take your place, Seldon," he replied to the Marquis, "you are very much mistaken. We have all tried, and failed. Instead, we hobble along behind you, grateful for the crumbs that fall from the rich man's table."

The Marquis laughed.

"You are very modest all of a sudden, and that, I may tell you, Neville, is not your reputation."

"I am merely envious," Lord Neville said. "I am also flattering you, Seldon, so that you will give me one of your best horses to ride in the Steeple-Chase. I have nothing in my own stable good enough to compete with yours, so if you want me to finish the course in style, you must provide me with the means to do it."

The Marquis had anticipated this, and he said:

"I have two horses for you to choose from, Neville, and I shall be interested to see which you prefer."

Lord Neville looked extremely satisfied at his host's reply. Then, as if he thought he must ingratiate himself further, he said to Lady Sinclair:

"Will you come tomorrow to help me choose the winner of this contest? I suppose you know that as well as the Challenge Cup there is a prize of two thousand guineas, which I could well do with at the moment."

"Are you seriously asking me to help you to defeat Seldon?" Lady Sinclair enquired. "It is useless, because he will win. He is too magnificent and too omnipotent to be defeated in any activity in which he competes seriously."

Her voice was very moving, but unfortunately the Marquis was no longer listening.

He had turned once again to Indira, only to find, to his annoyance, that she was talking to the gentleman on her other side.

He was a middle-aged but still raffish Peer who had a dull and conformable wife who never accompanied him to the Marquis's parties.

He was in consequence prepared to make the very most of his freedom.

"I do not believe," he was saying to Indira, "that anything so exquisite or so overwhelmingly beautiful as you could possibly have come from India or anywhere except Paris.

You have French *chic* written all over you, and an allure-
ment that has a special magic peculiar to French women and
is quite inimitable."

As he uttered the fulsome compliments he moved his face
nearer to Indira, and it made her recoil from him.

The Marquis was aware that she was repulsed in a way he
found hard to understand.

Without replying, she turned to him and he saw an expression of fear in her eyes, which surprised him.

He was intrigued, and yet he was too wise to refer to it, but
merely continued his conversation quietly on the subject of
books.

It was only when the gentlemen joined the ladies in the
Drawing-Room that the Marquis found himself, almost
without meaning to, gravitating towards Indira, who was
seated on a sofa near the fireplace.

Because it was still chilly in the evening and the storm
during the day had left a damp atmosphere outside, the fire
had been lit and Indira was glad of its warmth.

She was well aware that after a few desultory words when
they reached the Drawing-Room, the majority of the ladies
had left her alone while they gossiped amongst themselves.

Lady Sinclair in particular ignored her, while she made it
very clear to the other women who was the most important
person at the Marquis's party.

"Dear Seldon has arranged this Steeple-Chase especially
for me," she was saying in her child-like way. "It is the first
time that ladies have been allowed to ride with the men, and
it will be a great triumph if I can win. But of course, as you
know, Seldon likes to be first in everything."

"You mean we can ride too?" one of the ladies exclaimed.
"Why did the Marquis not tell us when we were invited? I
would have brought a horse with me who is a magnificent
jumper!"

"I am sure it would be a mistake for you to compete

except on your own horse," Lady Sinclair said quickly. "After all, the course will be very dangerous, and the jumps are very high."

"I am sure, dearest Rosie, if they are safe enough for you they will be safe for us," one of the ladies said in a spiteful voice, "unless you are doing a little bit of cheating by having special places in the fences made easy for you."

"I am sure dear Seldon would not do anything that was not completely honourable," Lady Sinclair replied, "and he considers me a very fine rider."

"Well, I think it is unfair that we were not told!" another lady insisted.

Indira, listening, thought with amusement that Lady Sinclair had definitely asserted herself in a way they seemed to resent.

She wondered if there was any chance of her riding one of Charles's or James's horses which they told her had been sent on ahead.

She had no idea how good Englishwomen were as eques-triennes, but she herself had ridden every sort of horse, including some very fine Arabian mares in Arabia.

She knew she would love to compete, not because she wanted the prize but for the thrill of jumping English fences and riding on an outstanding English horse.

She thought she would ask Charles or Jimmy about it as soon as they came from the Dining-Room, but the Marquis reached her first, and as he sat down on the sofa beside her she realised that he was a man, and instinctively, without questioning whether or not he would notice it, she moved away from him.

He did notice, and it surprised him.

He had never yet met a woman who was not eager to be as close to him as possible, and who sooner or later invariably irritated him by the way in which she made every excuse to touch him with her hands or to press her shoulder against him.

That any woman, and especially one as young and lovely as his new guest, should deliberately widen the distance between them made him want to ask her the reason for it.

Then as he looked at her he saw what appeared to be a flicker of fear in her strange eyes, which made him extremely curious.

Then as if she forced herself to think of something other than his sex, Indira said:

"The ladies are all talking of your Steeple-Chase, and I gather it is the first time they have been allowed to compete in it."

"Only over the first half, which is easier than what comes later," the Marquis replied. "Are you telling me that you would like to join it?"

There was a little silence before Indira said:

"It is something I would enjoy doing, and I have looked forward to riding in England, but I may not be good . . . enough . . . I do not know."

"You will have a chance tomorrow to see the course, and that will give you the answer better than I can."

"Can I really do that?" Indira asked eagerly.

The Marquis smiled.

"I can see it is going to be a choice between my stables and my Library, and I wonder which will win."

"If I were really forced to choose," Indira replied, "I should say the Library."

"I will be generous and allow you to sample both."

"Thank you . . . thank you . . . very much."

As Charles came up to join them, he wondered why Indira was looking so happy.

*

The following morning Indira came down to breakfast to find Charles alone in the Breakfast-Room.

"Am I late or early?" she asked, as he rose at her approach.

"Early," he replied. "You went to bed before midnight, which was very sensible of you. The rest of the party stayed up very late gambling and drinking far too much to make an early rise enjoyable."

"I had no idea you were going to gamble," Indira said. "I would like to have seen the tables."

"They were in the next room," Charles replied. "But what do you mean you would like to have seen the tables?"

"I have heard so much about gaming in England, and of course the Chinese play very different games, while the Indians prefer talking, which is usually about politics, and they become very heated on the subject!"

Charles laughed.

"I won a few pounds last night, then slipped off to bed. I wanted a clear head for the Steeple-Chase, which is what the Marquis always has."

Indira looked at him enquiringly, and he explained:

"He always wins his own Steeple-Chase, and I am convinced it is because he drinks very little and is extremely fit."

He lowered his voice as he said:

"Because he is an excellent host, his guests are stupid enough to indulge themselves at his expense. Too much claret does not make for good, hard riding, which we will all need if we are to finish the course."

"I want to ride too," Indira said.

"I heard a lot of talk last night about Lady Sinclair taking part in the race," Charles replied, "but I did not believe it."

"Her Ladyship is quite certain she is going to win."

"Then you must certainly beat her!" Charles said quickly. "You can have one of my horses. I have four with me."

"You must not give me the one you want for yourself," Indira replied. "And Lady Sinclair thinks she is very, very good. So please do not be disappointed if she beats me."

"What is all this?" asked Jimmy, who had come up behind them while they were talking.

"Indira is going to take part in the race, and I only hope she can ride well. We shall feel very guilty if she ends up with a broken neck."

"I can ride anything from a donkey to an elk," Indira said, "but what we are concerned with at the moment is a really good jumper. The Marquis has promised that I can see the course today."

"He did?" Charles exclaimed. "Well, if he offers you one of his horses—jump at the chance! They are superlative."

"I expect he is keeping the best for Lady Sinclair," Jimmy said, "and you realise that if Indira beats her, she will scratch her eyes out!"

Indira looked worried.

"I have no wish to upset her," she said, "and if she wants the Marquis to admire her riding, I will not compete."

"What we want," Charles said in a low voice, "is for him to admire you."

Indira helped herself from a silver dish that was offered her before she answered:

"What you are asking me to do is too difficult, and I think it would be wise to let me leave today."

"If you do that," Charles said sharply, "it will be most ungrateful, besides being very stupid from your own point of view."

Indira gave a little cry.

"I have no wish to be ungrateful. As you must know, I can never thank either of you . . . enough for all you have . . . done for me. It is just that I am . . . very bad at . . . intrigue."

As she spoke she was aware that the Marquis had come into the room.

He was looking magnificent in riding-clothes, and his boots were so highly polished that they seemed to reflect like mirrors.

Charles and Jimmy would have risen to their feet, but he said:

"No, please do not move! Good-morning, Lady Mary! I

am surprised to see you so early. The rest of my party will doubtless sleep late."

"Lady Mary is very anxious to enter the Steeple-Chase," Charles said, "but to tell you the truth, I am astonished that you are allowing women on the course. I should have thought the jumps were far too high for them."

"I have lowered the first ten," the Marquis replied, "but after that you will find the rest are more difficult than they have ever been."

The Marquis said no more while he refused two dishes which were offered to him and took a small spoonful from a third before he went on:

"Lady Mary is going to see the course this morning, and I know she will be sensible enough to withdraw from the contest if she thinks it is too much for her. If there is a female casualty, no woman will ever be allowed to jump at Ardsley Hall again."

"I promise you I will be very honest about my capabilities," Indira said, "but I find it frustrating to think that men are convinced that no woman can ever equal them in sport if in nothing else."

"How can they?" Jimmy asked before the Marquis could reply. "You can hardly have women jockeys or women gameshots. And how could a woman pugilist stand a chance?"

Charles laughed.

"That is certainly ludicrous! But riding is rather different, and some women ride extremely well."

"In Rotten Row!" Jimmy exclaimed scathingly. "Most of them in the hunting-field look for a gap in the hedge, or the nearest gate."

"You are talking rather scathingly, Overton," the Marquis said, "but I agree with you, women should not compete in men's sports or really in anything else."

"I see Your Lordship has Eastern ideas of women's place in the world," Indira remarked.

The way she challenged the Marquis made Charles look at Jimmy with a twinkle in his eyes.

They both knew Ardsley's views on women.

"Women," the Marquis replied a trifle ponderously, "should be beautiful to look at and entertaining to talk to, but they should certainly not encroach on what are traditionally male prerogatives. That of course includes strenuous games or anything that is dangerous."

He spoke positively and as if there could be no possible argument.

Indira did not reply, but there was a little smile on her lips before she said:

"If Your Lordship will be kind enough to let me see your horses and ride one before everybody else appears who will need your attention, I will go and change into a riding-habit so that I can be ready when you have finished your breakfast."

She did not wait for the Marquis to agree, but went quickly from the Breakfast-Room.

"I must congratulate you, Frodham," the Marquis said when she had gone. "You certainly played the 'Knight Errant' to a very charming and lovely young lady when you saved her from the Highwaymen."

"She is also very intelligent," Charles replied.

"So I discovered last night," the Marquis said, "and I shall be interested to see how she rides, but I expect I shall be disappointed. The type of animal that is available in Eastern countries could not be compared with the horses in our stables."

"No, of course not," Charles agreed. "At the same time, with this innovation of yours, women will at least have a chance to prove themselves as Amazons."

"I hope that will not be the case," the Marquis said sharply. "If there is one thing I really dislike, it is a hard-riding, hard-drinking woman! And that is unfortunately the species which is developing in Leicestershire and in some of the more fashionable Hunting Counties."

"I agree," Jimmy said. "A woman should be beautiful and feminine. At the same time, some of the Cyprians in London look very alluring in Hyde Park on the horses they ride for the Livery Stables."

There was a faint twist to the Marquis's lips as he remarked:

"I also have eyes in my head, Overton!"

"I thought you would not have missed them," Jimmy said quickly. "They cut quite a dash in their colourful habits."

"And in one's pocket!" Charles added ruefully.

As he spoke, he was thinking of one charmer for whom he had bought a very expensive horse, and when their liaison was over he learnt that she had sold it at a profit.

The Marquis finished his breakfast and said:

"I expect you will want to ride too, if we are going to the course. Have you ordered your horses?"

"I will do so at once," Charles replied.

He went from the Breakfast-Room and Jimmy followed him a few seconds later.

Charles was waiting for him in the Hall.

"I have ordered your horse as well as mine," he said. "I am hoping to God that Indira does not make a fool of herself. Things are going very well, and did you realise last night that Lady Sinclair was seething with rage because the Marquis paid her so much attention? She was happy only when Indira had gone to bed and she had him to herself again."

"If you ask me, she is on the way out," Jimmy said. "She is far too possessive with him, and I am sure he is intrigued with Indira, although it is too soon to hope for big results."

"Much too soon," Charles agreed positively.

He walked across the Hall and onto the steps to wait for the horses to be brought to the front door. Then he said:

"I wish now we had told Indira not to ride, but how were

we to know that the Marquis had changed his rules and was letting women in on the race?"

Before Jimmy could reply, the Marquis joined them, and at the same time they saw the horses being led down to the side of the house from the direction of the stables.

They were certainly magnificent to look at, their silver bridles glinting in the sunshine, and the horse with a side-saddle was a superlative animal, jet-black except for a white star on his nose.

Charles's horse and Jimmy's were both extremely well-bred, fine-looking horse-flesh which any man would be proud to own, but they could not compare with the magnificent stallion that belonged to the Marquis, and which seemed in its own way to be not only as majestic but also as dashing as he was.

The men were just descending the steps when Indira came running down behind them.

She was looking as alluring as Charles had hoped she would, and even more so, in a very smart summer habit of dark green pique edged with white braid.

The tight-fitting jacket gave her a tiny waist, and her high-crowned hat with its gauze veil trailing behind was extremely becoming.

Charles also noted that her hair was arranged as neatly as any woman might have worn it in the hunting-field, and he thought with a sigh of relief that it was something he had forgotten to tell her.

She might easily have appeared with untidy curls, ringlets, or some other type of coiffure which would have been taboo for any Lady of Quality.

He went towards her, but before he could get there the Marquis was before him, and putting his hands on each side of her waist he lifted her onto the side-saddle.

She placed her leg over the pummel, and with an experienced hand he arranged her skirts over the one stirrup.

She looked down at him and smiled.

"Thank you," she said. "Now will you kindly allow me to get acquainted with my horse, which is something I consider important if we are to show our paces together?"

She bent forward as she spoke, patting the horse's neck and talking to him in a quiet, almost mesmeric voice which made the animal twitch his ears as if he understood.

"I see you are experienced enough to know that is necessary," the Marquis said drily.

"It is especially necessary if one is riding a rampaging elephant or a racing camel!" Indira replied.

He laughed before he mounted his own horse, then they set off, moving slowly away from the house and into the Park.

"There are rabbit-holes here," the Marquis said, "as strangers learn to their cost, so hold in your horses until we are away from the trees."

Charles, however, was concentrating on Indira.

She seemed very much at home in the saddle, and he thought she looked extremely alluring and at the same time so graceful as to appear fragile. He was afraid that if the horse pulled, she might not be able to hold him.

It took them a little time to ride beneath the great oak trees to where on the other side of the Park there was meadowland, and the young grass was filled with cuckoo flowers and cowslips.

The Marquis looked at Indira and enquired:

"Would you like to give *Meteor* his head?"

"I hope he lives up to his name," she replied.

She did not wait for the Marquis to lead the way but touched *Meteor* very slightly with her heel. He sprang forward and Indira knew with a feeling of delight that she was riding a perfectly trained and exceptional animal.

She was well aware that all three men were appraising her and she made no attempt to ride more quickly than they were doing.

She merely let *Meteor* take his pace from the Marquis, and

they galloped without trying to race each other for nearly a mile.

Then the Marquis turned his horse and said:

"The Steeple-Chase is a little below us. You can see the beginning of it and the first fences from here."

They all pulled in their horses and the Marquis showed them how he had laid out his Steeple-Chase on some flat fields where he had erected fences which to Charles and Jimmy from that distance did not appear to be very formidable.

"Shall we go down and try them?" the Marquis asked.

They followed him to the beginning of the course. The fences were broad, with plenty of room for all four horses to have jumped them together, but because they knew it was a test, both Charles and Jimmy stood back to let the Marquis and Indira go ahead.

Meteor leapt over the fences almost disdainfully, and at the end of the first five the Marquis drew in his horse to say:

"Now this is where the ladies break away from the male riders. They will turn to the left and jump another five fences which are equivalent to the ones we have just taken. Then they will have a guide to lead them across country so that they can be at the winning-post, where the men will finish, about two miles from here."

"It sounds very gruelling," Charles said.

"When you see the rest of the fences, you will realise that is the right word," the Marquis said with a smile.

"What happens if a lady wins the Steeple-Chase?" Jimmy asked.

"You can surely not accuse me of being parsimonious when it comes to racing," the Marquis answered mockingly. "Instead of a Cup, the winning lady will receive a necklace, which I may tell you is a very attractive one, and I am splitting the two thousand guineas into two portions, male and female, which you must admit is permissible in the circumstances."

"I am sure the winning lady will consider it an achieve-ment, not because of the prizes, but because she has per-suaded the noble Marquis to initiate something which puts her on almost equal terms with him."

The way in which Indira spoke made the Marquis look surprised, and Charles gave her a warning glance. Then she said quickly, as if she felt she had said too much:

"At the same time, I think it is a wonderful idea and very encouraging for the women, who are always kept out of anything competitive."

The Marquis moved his horse to her side.

"I have the feeling, Lady Mary, that you are jeering at me!"

"No, no, of course not, My Lord," Indira replied. "And I hope that you will . . . allow me to . . . compete in your . . . Steeple-Chase."

"Having seen the way you took those jumps on *Meteor,* how could I possibly refuse?"

"Thank you."

As Indira spoke she deliberately turned her horse, and he had the strange feeling that while she was excited about the race, she disliked him being close to her.

Chapter Four

THE Marquis, having changed his clothes after riding, came down the stairs aware that there was a murmur of voices in the Drawing-Room.

He thought he recognised Lady Sinclair's child-like tone and decided that he did not wish to encounter her at the moment.

He was quite certain she would be reproachful and plaintive because he had been riding without her, and would be exceedingly jealous when she realised that he had been accompanied by Lady Mary.

If there was one thing that bored the Marquis, it was women who became excessively jealous when they had no reason for it. Before he reached the Hall he had come to the conclusion that he had finished with Lady Sinclair.

The suddennesss of his decision surprised him, for usually in his many and fiery love-affairs there was a "cooling off" period before he finally made up his mind that he was bored and had no intention of continuing a liaison which no longer interested him.

He was quite ruthless where women were concerned, for the simple reason that he had no respect for married women who betrayed their husbands with him or with anybody else.

It was a sentiment that would certainly have surprised his contemporaries if he had confided in them, but as he had long ago told himself, his principles, if that was what they were, were out-of-date and quite ridiculous.

Nevertheless, every time he went into another man's house to find his wife waiting eagerly for him, her arms outstretched, her lips lifted to him, he despised himself and the woman in question.

Then he told himself that although he had mistresses like every other Gentleman of Quality—it was in its way the same as owning superlative horses or fine paintings—these women were not of any great importance in his life and were very easily dispensable.

Had he had anything to do with young girls, it would have meant, as he was acutely aware, being hurried up the aisle by her parents, ambitious to have the most eligible and certainly the richest bachelor in the country as a son-in-law.

The result was that his leisure hours were inevitably spent with married women who were cuckolding their husbands, and it was part of the scene set by the Prince Regent, whose mistress at the moment was the Marchioness of Hertford.

That her husband was not only complaisant but pleased with the arrangement made the Marquis regard him scornfully and remark to one of his friends:

"Hertford wags his tail round Carlton House like an excited terrier!"

He thought as he crossed the Hall that Lord Sinclair, who had found another "interest," and a very pretty one at that, would doubtless be summoned home to escort his wife until she found another lover.

It did not worry him what either Lord or Lady Sinclair thought. But he knew that he would find it difficult to avoid a scene before his guests returned to London on Monday.

As it was something he invariably encountered when an *affaire de coeur* was at an end, he metaphorically shrugged his shoulders and told himself that Rosie, as she was well bred, would behave like a Lady.

At the same time, he had the uncomfortable feeling that blue blood did not always ensure self-control!

In his experience, women were so distraught at losing his affection that they would not only scream and cry but would threaten suicide in an effort to blackmail him back into their arms.

He thought mockingly that it would have been far more convenient from his point of view if his decision about Rosie Sinclair had not been made so soon after her arrival at Ardsley Hall.

But he knew without argument that the curtain had fallen, and when he saw her again she would not even seem as beautiful as she had when he had invited her to take part in his Steeple-Chase.

It was something he had been very reluctant to do, but becaue she was a good rider she had pleaded with him at an intimate moment when it would have been very difficult for a man to refuse any request from a very beautiful woman.

'Let us hope she wins,' he thought to himself. 'The necklace will soothe her feelings better than words.'

He knew he was being over-optimistic, for no necklace, however magnificent, however expensive, could compensate a woman for losing him.

In reality he was not as conceited as his enemies thought, and he often found it a handicap rather than an asset that women found him irresistible as a lover, which, when combined with his aura of wealth and prestige, made him outstanding in the society in which he moved.

He had almost reached his Study, where he knew he would find the newspapers which he intended to read before luncheon, when he thought it was likely that Lady Mary would be in the Library.

She had ridden back to the house ahead of him, and he had known, although he had found it difficult to understand, that she had no wish to talk to him intimately, as any other woman would have done.

She had attached herself to Charles Frodham and quite obviously preferred his company.

The Marquis wondered for a moment if because he had

rescued her from the Highwaymen, Lady Mary had fallen in love with the young man.

Yet, he was perceptive enough to realise that her attitude towards both Charles Frodham and James Overton was that of a sister for a brother.

He was too experienced with women not to know when there was that little glint in the eyes, that flirtatious curve of the lips, or the vibrations which made a man aware that she was very conscious of his masculinity.

But there was nothing like that about Lady Mary when she talked to the two young men who had brought her to Ardsley Hall, and where the rest of the male guests and himself were concerned, the Marquis was now sure that when they came near her she was actually afraid.

It was something he had never encountered before; in fact, he could not remember in the whole of his life any woman being afraid of him.

'If anything,' he thought cynically, 'the boot is on the other foot!'

Even when he was very young, women had pursued him, and his self-assurance came from having made love to so many, a great number of whom had chased him rather than allow him to do his own hunting.

Just as he had said at White's, he told himself now that women were all the same.

And yet he knew that Lady Mary was different, and he wished to know why.

He opened the door of the Library, and as he did so he heard her voice from the far end of the room say:

"Please . . . leave me alone . . . I want to read this book, which I find very . . . interesting."

There was undoubtedly a quiver of fear in the way she spoke.

The Marquis could not see her because all down the room bookcases jutted out from the wall, and she was behind one

which he knew contained the Chinese volume about which
he had spoken to her.

"I have no intention of leaving you alone," a man replied,
and the Marquis recognised that it belonged to Lord
Wrotham, who had sat next to her at dinner the night
before.

When he realised that Wrotham was upsetting her, he
had thought that it had been a mistake to place him beside
her because he was a notorious womaniser who continually
boasted of his successes.

However, the Marquis's party had been planned to con-
tain only his personal friends, and those did not include
young, unmarried women.

"I have been dreaming about you all night," Lord
Wrotham was saying, "and counting the hours until I could
see you again."

Indira did not reply, and he asked:

"How can you be so beautiful? You are a temptation to
every man who looks at you, and all I am asking, my little
temptress, is that you will be a little kind to me."

"Please . . . go away!" Indira replied.

Then she gave a scream.

"Do not . . . dare to . . . touch me . . . you have no right
. . ."

She screamed again, and the Marquis realised that this
could not be allowed.

He hurried down the room, making his footsteps as loud
as possible as a warning to Lord Wrotham.

As he came round the end of the bookcase, it was to see
Indira with her back against the books, and Lord Wrotham,
having obviously just taken his hands from her, looked
round angrily at being interrupted.

"So here you are, Wrotham!" the Marquis said slowly,
drawling his words as if he was in no hurry. "One of the
servants is looking for you. I think he has a message."

"A message?" Lord Wrotham exclaimed. "I cannot think what it might be."

"You will find the man in the Hall."

Lord Wrotham muttered something beneath his breath and walked past the Marquis and up the Library towards the door.

Only when he had gone did the Marquis look directly at Indira to see an expression of terror in her eyes.

She was clasping a book to her breast with both hands, as if to calm the tumult within her, and he realised that her whole body was trembling.

"I am sorry he upset you," he said quietly.

For a moment she did not reply. Then she said:

"They . . . promised . . . because I am . . . unmarried . . . that this . . . would not happen."

The Marquis looked puzzled and asked:

"Who promised?"

"Charles . . . and James . . . please . . . I cannot stay . . . I want to go away!"

The Marquis did not answer, and she said with a violence which was different from the way she had been speaking before:

"I hate men! I hate . . . them all! I must go . . . into a . . . Convent! There is . . . nowhere else where I can be . . . safe."

The Marquis was completely astounded. Then he said:

"I think you are upset because of what happened yester-day, and I am sorry Wrotham should have behaved in such a stupid manner. But it is one of the penalties you have to pay for being such a very beautiful woman!"

"I hate . . . my hair! I hate my . . . face!" Indira cried desperately. "If I were ugly they would leave me . . . alone . . . and that is all I . . . want."

"I think every ugly woman would give her right arm to look as you do," the Marquis said with a faint smile.

"I am . . . going into a . . . Convent," Indira said de-cidedly. "Please . . . tell me where I can . . . find one . . . and where they will . . . admit me if I promise to become a . . . Catholic."

The Marquis looked at her to see if she was really sincere.

He prided himself that he always knew if a man or woman was lying, and he was aware that Indira was telling the truth and she really intended to do as she said.

"I would never have imagined," he said slowly after a moment's pause, "that riding as you do, and having a very intelligent brain, you would be a coward!"

Indira started and looked at him almost as if he had slapped her or thrown cold water in her face.

He was aware that he had given her a shock, and she was no longer trembling.

"I am not . . . really a . . . coward," she said after a moment, as if she spoke to herself. "Papa would be . . . ashamed of me if I were."

"I am sure your father would be very ashamed if he thought you would do anything so absurd as to imprison yourself in a Convent just because you have not the courage to face the world as it is."

"But . . . men will not . . . leave me . . . alone."

The Marquis thought it was what most women longed and prayed for, but he said:

"All men are not like Wrotham, and I promise you while he is here in my house he will not trouble you again."

"I . . . think I would rather . . . leave."

"I cannot prevent you from doing so, but I should be very disappointed."

As he spoke, Indira remembered that she not only had nowhere to go, but if she left Charles and Jimmy behind, she would have no protection from Mr. Jacobson.

Lord Wrotham was certainly very frightening, but it was also frightening to think of going alone to London and trying to find somewhere to stay until she found which of her relations were alive and willing to welcome her.

Almost as if the Marquis could read her thoughts he said:

"As I understand it, you have at the moment nobody to travel with, and as you have been through some worrying and shocking experiences, would it not be wiser to give yourself a chance to consider your next move?"

Indira did not speak and he went on:

"I am sure Frodham and Overton will escort you if you wish to go to London when you leave here, but it would be very selfish if you left today and prevented them from taking part in my Steeple-Chase."

Indira gave a deep sigh.

"I am sure ... My Lord, that I am being ... selfish and foolish ... but please ... please do not let that man come ... near me again! He touched me ... and he was trying ... to kiss me!"

"I have already promised," the Marquis said, "that he will behave himself in the future. I can only apologise that one of my guests should have behaved so outrageously in my house."

He knew as he spoke that it was not really an unusual occurrence at Ardsley Hall, and despite Lady Mary's explanations as to why she was travelling alone, Wrotham might easily have misconstrued it and convinced himself that her family was not particularly concerned with her.

Such a beautiful young woman would not usually be allowed anywhere without an elderly and competent Chaperone.

Now for the first time the Marquis found the whole situation rather strange.

He had accepted the story of her not being met at Southampton without query simply because it had not occurred to him to suspect there to be anything unusual about it.

Now he could think of a great number of questions he would like to ask, but he knew it was something he could not do while Indira was still upset.

"What I am going to suggest," he said in a voice that was calm, impersonal, and, he hoped, reassuring, "is that you forget what has happened, and in the short time we have before luncheon let us discuss together the book you are holding in your hand, which I came here to find for you."

"I looked in the . . . catalogue on the . . . table," Indira replied.

There was still a tremor in her voice, but the Marquis knew she was making an effort to do what he wished.

For the first time since they had been talking she took the book away from her breast and looked down at it.

"You are very . . . very . . . fortunate to . . . possess this," she said.

"That is what I have always thought myself," the Marquis replied. "But I assure you that very few of my guests appreciate its age or what it contains."

"But you had it . . . translated?"

"No, that was done by my grandfather," the Marquis replied, "who was clever enough to know how valuable it was, and to employ the greatest scholars of his time to translate it."

"I have heard of 'The Song of Lo Fu,'" Indira said, looking down at the book, "but I like best the little poem by Li Po."

The Marquis was just about to move to her side to look down at the pages of the translation that she held in her hand. Then he thought it might frighten her if he stood too close, and instead he said:

"I have not read it for some years, so suppose you read it to me?"

Indira gave him a little smile.

"I will just read the last three lines," she said.

> *How many times has the rose flowered?*
> *Do the white clouds as then scatter themselves?*
> *And behind whose dwelling sets the moon?*

The Marquis thought her voice was very soft, and the

words seemed to speak to her of the world behind the world.

As if she knew that was what he thought, she said:

"I studied with a Chinese Philosopher, and he taught me that each one of us finds a different meaning in what we read."

"Come with me," the Marquis said. "I will show you something which I am sure you will appreciate."

Indira put the book into its place on the shelf and walked with him to another part of the Library.

There in the centre of the wall was a Chinese cabinet of red lacquer raised above a carved and gilt stand.

It was very beautiful and she had meant to examine it after she had looked at the book, knowing that it was something her father would have enjoyed and that she herself would love to own it.

The Marquis unlocked the doors to the cabinet with a gold key and drew from one of the drawers inside something wrapped in silk.

From it he took out a pottery model of a prancing horse and held it out to Indira.

She gave a little cry of delight.

"A T'ang Dynasty horse!" she exclaimed. "How can you be so lucky as to possess anything so wonderful?"

"It was given to me by my grandfather when I became twenty-one, and he had been given it by his father," the Marquis replied.

Indira touched its glazed surface with the tip of her fingers.

"Only the craftsmen of the T'ang Dynasty," she said as if she spoke to herself, "could catch the vigour and tension of an animal in motion."

"That is what I thought," the Marquis agreed.

"My teacher said," Indira said, her eyes on the horse, "that the sculptured art of the T'ang Dynasty is entirely confident of its mastery of the faith and ability to express vitality and strength of the visual form."

Then as she spoke, thinking of the horse, she thought that might also apply to the Marquis, and a faint flush rose in her cheeks.

Suddenly he was aware that he could read her thoughts, and he told himself that he had never had a more sincere or more unexpected compliment.

And yet in a way he could understand that to somebody as perceptive as Indira, the T'ang Dynasty horse she held in her hands with its expression of pride and vigour was undoubtedly what he aimed for in himself.

Indira stroked the arched neck of the horse, then she gave it back to the Marquis with a little sigh, saying:

"Thank you. I have never seen a more perfect example of T'ang sculpture. I feel that although we know it was originally a tomb figure, it actually lives."

The Marquis took the horse from her, wrapped it again in its silk shroud, and replaced it very carefully in the drawer.

"I think we both know from our studies," he said, "that there is no such thing as death, only life in different spheres."

He was not looking at her as he shut the lacquered doors of the cabinet, but he was aware that she was sta
ing at him wide-eyed before she said in a voice that seemed to vibrate between them:

"How could I have been so stupid as not to realise that before? Of course you are right! I have not lost . . . Papa, he is . . . still with me!"

The Marquis turned to look at her and saw that her eyes were shining almost as if there were a star hidden in their depths.

Then without saying anything more she turned and went from the Library. He knew that she felt for the moment as if she must be alone and could not speak to anybody of what she was feeling.

As he stood there, thinking it was the strangest and most unexpected conversation he had ever had with a woman, what Indira had just said came back into his mind.

"I have not lost Papa, he is still with me!"

Thinking back, he could not remember there having been anything said last night on her arrival about Lord Farncombe being dead, and he was quite sure that it had not been reported in the newspapers.

The Marquis was very precise in his reading, as he was in everything else, and when the newspapers arrived he read the headlines, the Editorials, the Parliamentary Reports, then the Court Columns and the Obituaries of distinguished people, which were printed on the same page.

He was therefore convinced that there had been no mention of the death of the Earl of Farncombe, whom he had never met, but who he was well aware was spoken of highly when people talked of India.

Ever since the victories of Colonel Wellesley—now the Duke of Wellington—at the end of the last century and the rapid expansion of British control of India, it was a frequent topic of conversation in the House of Lords and at the Foreign Office, where the Marquis was often entertained.

He was now quite convinced that there was something strange about Lady Mary and the circumstances which had brought her to Ardsley Hall.

It was something he could not exactly put into words, but it was a tangled skein which he was determined to unravel, and he found himself interested and intrigued in a way he had not been for a very long time.

He joined his guests in the Drawing-Room, and Indira reappeared just before luncheon was announced.

As the Marquis watched her come through the door, he thought for a second that she looked different.

Then he realised it was because for the first time since she had been in his house, she was not looking worried, tense, or apprehensive, but happy.

*

When Indira went to bed that night, early because she wanted a good night's rest before the Steeple-Chase the next day, she lay thinking how extremely fortunate she had been in coming to Ardsley Hall.

She could not explain to herself now why she had been so foolish in giving way to the despair and misery which had encompassed her like a cloud after her father's death.

She had loved him so deeply and he had meant so much in her life that when he died she felt as if part of herself had gone with him and she was no longer a whole person.

She was sensible enough to know that the shock from which she was suffering was mainly physical, and now she was ashamed and in a way humiliated that her beliefs and her faith, which had glowed like a light, had been tried to the point where she had not applied to her personal sorrow all she had learnt.

She had not realised, as she did now, that her father was not dead but was near her, loving her and being part of her as he had always been.

"How can I have been so idiotic, Papa," she asked in the darkness, "as to have forgotten all we talked about so often? And we both know . . . how much it guided your life . . . and of course . . . mine."

It seemed extraordinary that it should have been left to a perfect stranger, and of all people the cynical, supercilious Marquis of Ardsley, to reveal the truth to her.

Now, as if he had lit a blazing light to show her the way, the clouds had vanished and she could see, hear, and think, and she was no longer unhappy or even afraid.

Looking back, she supposed it was immediately after her father's Funeral, which had taken place within six hours of his death, that she became aware of being menaced by the people who surrounded her.

The burial at sea was very moving and many of the passengers wept in sympathy, although Indira had remained dry-eyed and calm until she was alone.

Then she wept tempestuously, not only at the misery of losing somebody she loved so deeply, but also at the terror of being alone.

After that, everything had seemed a little muddled and indistinct, as if she moved in a fog, and she felt as if everything that happened was a nightmare from which she could not awaken.

'How could I not have tried to reach Papa with my prayers and the vibrations that always existed between us?' Indira thought, and felt as if he was now near her, as he had not been since she believed he had died.

"I am not alone! I am not alone!" she said to herself. "Papa is here, thinking of me, guiding me, protecting me!"

She was quite sure now that it was her father who had helped her to escape from the Hotel and Mr. Jacobson, and who had brought Charles and Jimmy to her rescue.

Also undoubtedly he had brought her to Ardsley Hall so that she should learn how foolish she had been.

She could feel the T'ang horse beneath her fingers, and she knew it was that even more than the Marquis's words which had reminded her that life is eternal and death nothing more than the shedding of an unwanted garment.

"I understand now, Papa, and I am no longer afraid. I am sorry, very sorry that I failed you, and myself, in such a foolish manner."

She felt as if her father was smiling at her, and she could feel the power of the faith in which they both believed seeping back into her and driving out the last remnants of doubt and fear.

"How could I ever have thought of imprisoning myself in a Convent?" she asked herself. "I should have been thinking of ways in which I could spend the money you left me for the benefit of other people."

At the same time, now that her brain was functioning clearly, she knew it was going to be hard to know exactly what she could do in a country which, while she belonged to it, was as strange to her as if she had suddenly found herself living on the moon.

'I must find Papa's relations, and I am sure they will help me,' she thought.

She wondered if perhaps her father's Bankers might be able to help her. Then she remembered that everything in England was in the hands of the firm of Solicitors whom he had trusted.

In any case, Indira was sure that no Solicitors, however honourable, would be the right people to advise her on the spending of her fortune.

Then an idea came to her which made her stare blankly into the darkness.

It was that the one person who could really help her and advise her was the Marquis.

"No, no, of course not!" she said aloud. "He is the last person who must know who I am. To tell him would be to betray Charles and Jimmy, who have been so kind to me."

At the same time, it was difficult not to remember that it was the Marquis and his T'ang Dynasty horse who had not only pointed the way but brought her peace of mind and the courage she should never have lost.

*

The next morning was bright and sunny, and Indira rose earlier than usual because she was not only excited at the idea of the Steeple-Chase but also, although she would not have admitted it to herself, eager to see the Marquis again.

She had awakened several times during the night to think about him, and found it extraordinary that a man she had come to the house prepared to despise and dislike had instead been the guide, the Guru, which every student of Eastern religion knows appears whenever the pupil is ready.

She thought it would be impossible to explain to Charles or Jimmy what had happened, and she would certainly not attempt it.

But when she had least expected it, the Guru had come, and although she thought that the Marquis would be totally unaware of it and would certainly not be interested, he had during those few minutes in the Library changed her whole attitude towards the future.

Because of what she had learnt in the East she did not for one moment question that this was what had happened or suspect that what had occurred was just chance.

It had all happened in a calm, mysterious way, but the pattern was there. The path that for a time had been twisting and indistinct had still to be followed, and now she was no longer indecisive but determined to go ahead.

'I want to talk to him, and perhaps there are other things he could tell me,' she thought.

At the same time, she was well aware that today of all days the Marquis would not be thinking of her, but of his Steeple-Chase and the many people who would be arriving to take part in it.

When she was dressed, wearing a riding-habit which had come from Paris and which because it was the deep blue of the sea made her skin dazzlingly white and her hair vivid as a flame, Indira went down to breakfast.

She had expected that nobody would be down so early and was therefore surprised to see the Marquis there, and as he rose to his feet at her entrance she exclaimed:

"I did not think anybody would be as early as I am!"

"When I am planning anything as important as a Steeple-Chase," he replied, "I find there are always difficulties at the last moment which have been overlooked, and even fences erected in the wrong way unless I inspect them."

Indira sat down at the table beside him and he said:

"I hope *Meteor* carries you to victory."

"I hope so too," Indira replied. "Last night I dreamt I was riding your T'ang Dynasty horse, but instead of galloping over the ground he flew with me towards the moon."

"I suppose that was the influence of the poem, and of course the horse himself," the Marquis said, and after a moment added:

"I too thought about the poem you read to me and tried to sort out the picture it made in my mind."

The Marquis's lips twisted a little before he went on:

"It is something I have not done since I was at Oxford, and I feel as if you have rolled back the years for me. Everything I thought then has become important again, almost as if it was waiting for my return."

"My teacher would have said that when we leave the path, whether by . . . mistake or . . . deliberately," Indira said in a low voice, "the path does not change but waits until we find out the . . . mistake we have made and go . . . back."

The Marquis was about to reply, but at that moment the door opened and Charles came into the room

"Good-morning, Ardsley!" he said to the Marquis. "Good-morning, Indira! You are very early!"

"What did you call Lady Mary just then?" the Marquis enquired in surprise.

"Jimmy and I call her by her second name because she has been in India," Charles replied, "and anyway, I think it is far more attractive than 'Mary,' which is somewhat ordinary."

"I agree with you," Indira said quickly, realising that he had made a mistake in the way he had addressed her. "It was my mother who chose 'Indira,' and she thought it very appropriate because my father loved everything that was

Indian, and they became engaged when they were in Simla."

The Marquis did not say anything. He merely thought this was another link in the puzzle he was trying to solve.

Then other guests appeared for breakfast, all of them men.

The Marquis finished and left the room, and Charles, sitting next to Indira, said:

"I want to talk to you. It was impossible last night after dinner to have a moment alone."

"Yes, I know," Indira replied, "and anyway, I went to bed early."

"You were very sensible," Charles said, "and actually Jimmy and I did not stay up late. I may not win, but I am determined to complete the course."

Jimmy sat down on the other side of Indira.

"We shall be lucky if we do," he remarked. "The jumps are far higher than they were last year."

"I expect there will be some casualties," Charles said, "but I am sure my horse can manage them."

"I would like to have a look at them before we start," Indira said. "Is that possible?"

"Of course it is," Charles replied, "and it is what I want to do myself. We do not want to hang about making desultory conversation with all the other competitors who are already starting to arrive."

"No, of courst not," Indira agreed.

She went upstairs and put on her riding-hat and boots and came down again to find Charles and Jimmy waiting for her in the Hall.

As they walked down the steps to where their horses were waiting for them, Charles said:

"I have just thought of something. I do not want to spoil your fun, but I think it is sensible."

"What is it?" Indira asked.

"Seeing the way you ride, and with the horse the Marquis

has lent you, you have every chance of beating Lady Sinclair or any other lady. But I think it would be a mistake."

"Why?"

"Because," Charles said, "not only will Lady Sinclair make a scene, but also an event like this is sure to be reported in the Social Columns of the newspapers."

"I never thought of that!" Jimmy exclaimed.

"Well, I have," Charles said, "and if Lady Mary Combe is the acclaimed winner of the Ardsley Hall Steeple-Chase, the Farncombe relations might ask why she is here without their knowledge, and try to get in touch with her."

"You are very sensible," Indira said, "so I promise you I will not beat Lady Sinclair. She can have all the honour and glory she wants."

"I am sorry," Charles said. "It seems extremely unfair, and I would not mind betting a considerable sum that you could win."

"It is important for me to ride but not particularly to win," Indira said with a smile.

They reached the horses and she patted *Meteor* and made a fuss of him.

He nuzzled his nose against her and she said in a voice only he could hear:

"You are very beautiful, but not quite as beautiful as the horse I was riding last night."

She was smiling at her own fantasy as Charles lifted her into the saddle, and when he and Jimmy were mounted they rode off to look at the course.

They went slowly, aware that the horses were restless and longing to gallop, but they kept them on a tight rein.

Already there were a number of people gathering in the meadow, and the Marquis's employees were putting the finishing touches to the hedges under his supervision.

They did not ride up to him but went instead onto the higher ground, so that they could see the whole course below them.

"You jump the smaller fences," Jimmy said to Indira, "then come on to the winning-post to watch Charles and me trailing valiantly behind the Marquis!"

"Do you think he will win?" Indira asked.

"Of course he will!" Jimmy said. "there can be no question about that, but I would like to be second."

"That is my place," Charles exclaimed, "and do not dare to do me out of it!"

"I bet you ten pounds I am ahead of you," Jimmy said.

Indira gave a little laugh.

"No, no, you must never bet on yourself. It is unlucky . . . at least, that is what my father always thought."

"Very well," Jimmy said, "but second is where I intend to be."

"You are becoming as self-satisfied and as sure of yourself as Ardsley!" Charles complained mockingly.

They joked with each other for a little while, then Jimmy said he wanted to ride down to look at the last few fences to make sure he took them in style.

He left Charles and Indira alone, and when he had gone Charles asked:

"I may be wrong, but you do not seem quite as worried as you were when we arrived."

"I am all right, thank you," Indira answered, "and I am ashamed of myself for letting two despicable men like Mr. Jacobson and Lord Wrotham upset me."

"Wrotham?" Charles exclaimed. "What has he done? He is a roué, and you are to have nothing to do with him!"

"I thought it would be a mistake to do so," Indira said demurely.

She felt there would be no point in telling Charles what had happened, because she was aware last night that the Marquis had kept his word and prevented Lord Wrotham from coming near her again.

She thought that he glared at her from across the room,

but she was no longer afraid because she was quite sure
he would not disobey the Marquis's orders to leave her
alone.

Now she could see the Marquis below her, riding from
one fence to the other and obviously giving orders, which
were quickly obeyed.

She was watching him so intently that she started when
Charles said:

"I suppose you realise how magnificent you have been
and that the Marquis is captivated by you."

"What makes you think that?"

"I know by the way he looks at you, for one thing,"
Charles answered, "and for another, the way Lady Sinclair
was behaving last night made it very obvious which way the
wind is blowing."

"I do not . . . understand."

"The Marquis was quite obviously ignoring her, and
when she asked him to come and sit next to her at the
gaming-table, he deliberately walked in the opposite direction, and she went white with fury."

"I am sorry for her if that is how she . . . feels about . . .
him."

Indira hesitated before she added:

"But . . . if she has a husband . . . surely it is . . . wrong?"

"I suppose it is," Charles said, "but you must realise that it
is a feather in any woman's cap to be able to say that she has
captivated, if only for a few months, the elusive Marquis of
Ardsley!"

Indira did not answer, and after a moment he said:

"What is important is that you have played your part to
the point where I am quite certain that when you leave on
Monday, Ardsley will make it clear that he wants to see you
again, and perhaps say even more than that."

"When do you intend to . . . tell him that I am . . . not
Lady Mary Combe?" Indira asked in a strange voice.

"I have not yet sorted out the ending of this drama," Charles replied, "but we have tomorrow yet to come."

He smiled, and there was a note of triumph in his voice as he said:

"Make no mistake, Indira, I shall have won my bet. We will have been at Ardsley Hall for three days, and not for one moment, I am quite certain, has the Marquis doubted that you were anything other than what you appear to be."

"I would not be . . . too sure of . . . that," Indira said in a low voice.

Then, to Charles's surprise, without waiting for him she started to ride down the hill towards Jimmy.

Chapter Five

LUNCHEON was early and the competitors were all entertained by the Marquis in the big Dining-Room.

There was a buffet, and drinks of every description, including champagne, were provided for his other guests in the Ball-Room.

When Indira, Charles, and Jimmy rode back to the house, coaches were already arriving to line the course, and the spectators had brought elaborate picnic-baskets which were being unpacked by liveried footmen.

"The Marquis certainly does everything in a slap-up manner!" Jimmy remarked.

"I can see it is very exciting for people who live in this part of the country to have a race-meeting all to themselves," Indira said.

As she spoke she was thinking that it was rather like the races in India which she had attended with her father, where huge crowds would gather to cheer on the jockeys and there was wild enthusiasm when a favourite won.

She had also often raced her father when they went riding every morning, and as he had horses imported from Arabia and from Europe that she was used to well-bred animals, although she thought that few of them had been quite as fine as *Meteor* and the stallion which the Marquis was riding.

When they arrived back at the house it was to find Lady Sinclair holding Court and looking exceedingly attractive in a black habit which displayed her pink-and-white-and-gold beauty better than any colour would have done.

She looked at Indira disdainfully and said in an audible voice:

"I always think black is the most suitable habit for anybody who rides seriously. Colours are far too theatrical."

Indira pretended not to hear her and tried not to laugh when Charles whispered: "Meaow-meaow!" at what he had overheard.

When she went in to luncheon she found that the Marquis had thought of her as he had last night, and she was seated not beside strangers but with Charles on her right-hand side and Jimmy on her left.

When she found her place she looked down the table and met his eyes, and she thought he understood that she was thanking him silently for being so considerate.

Because he had so many competitors to entertain, the majority of whom were men, she had assumed he would be too busy even to give her a thought.

But once or twice she realised that he was looking at her, and she hoped that he was not being critical because she was making no effort to entertain anybody except the two men with whom she had arrived at his house.

Lady Sinclair, on the other hand, constituted herself the Marquis's hostess and was showing off in a way that made it obvious that she wished everybody to know that she had a special position in the Marquis's household.

Indira could not help feeling that it was very wrong for her to parade her affection for him and his for her, when she already had a husband, and if Lord Sinclair had been there it would have been an humiliation for him to see his wife in such a role.

Then she told herself that it was not for her to find fault, especially as she was pretending to be somebody she was not and was deliberately deceiving the Marquis.

"Before I leave I will write a letter of apology, but I do not expect I shall ever see him again," she told herself.

The thought was depressing. She told herself it was because she had no friends in England, and she would have liked to feel that the Marquis was a friend and that she could see him again.

Yet she was quite certain that he would have no time for her, for not only was Lady Sinclair fawning on him in a way that seemed almost embarrassing, but other lady riders, two of whom were particularly beautiful, were doing exactly the same thing.

There were, however, only ten women competitors in all, and when luncheon was over and they rode down to the race-course, Charles said:

"Do not be nervous. I am sure you ride better than any of these other females, and you certainly have a finer horse."

"It was very kind of His Lordship to lend me *Meteor*," Indira said. "I feel we understand each other, and you will not be ashamed of me."

"We could never be that," Jimmy said impulsively. "You have been absolutely splendid, and the reason why Lady Sinclair has been behaving like a Prima Donna all through luncheon is because she is jealous of you."

"I cannot think why."

Charles was about to tell her the reason, when he thought that she might be embarrassed and it would spoil her chances in the race.

He had said to Jimmy last night when they went up to bed:

"You know, we really drew a winning card when we encountered Indira in that strange manner. Who would have thought that not only is she beautiful and extremely intelligent, but she rides better than any woman I have ever seen!"

"I was thinking the same thing," Jimmy said, "and if Ardsley is not infatuated with her he damned well ought to be!"

"I think he is," Charles answered, "but he is a strange man, and it is difficult to know what he is thinking."

"I am beginning to think I will lose my money," Jimmy said with a smile, "but it has been worth it. It has certainly given a spice to our visit which I did not expect."

"Nor I," Charles answered, "and, Jimmy, if I am honest, I would like to pursue Indira after we have found her somewhere to live."

"Why not?" Jimmy asked idly.

There was silence. Then Charles said:

"The truth is, I am afraid I am falling in love! So, as I do not wish to have a broken heart, the first thing I am going to do is to find another, 'Clarice' to amuse me, and forget her."

"I suppose, even though she is so rich, your family would not waive their prejudice against a tradesman's daughter?"

Charles gave a laugh which had no humour in it.

"You do not know my family," he said. "They are so stiff-necked, so certain that the earth was made for them to walk on, that they are as bad if not worse than Ardsley."

"Impossible!" Jimmy exclaimed, and they both laughed.

"How are we going to tell him we have made a fool of him?" Jimmy asked after a moment.

"I do not know," Charles said slowly. "I would hate to do anything which would be an embarrassment to Indira, and I think the best thing would be to wait until we have left, then write a letter apologising for deceiving him. We can be quite honest about it and say it was a bet."

Jimmy gave a cry of horror.

"You must be crazy! Ardsley will never forgive us, and we will never be asked here again."

"Well, you think of a better way," Charles said sharply. "After all, we cannot have gone to all this trouble for nothing."

Jimmy thought about it for a moment. Then he said:

"I suppose the only other way would be to say that Indira deceived us, but that seems rather mean."

"And definitely unsporting!" Charles said. "Ardsley has a great deal of power, and he might make himself unpleasant to her, and we can hardly allow that."

"No, of course not!" Jimmy agreed quickly.

They thought for a long time before finally they went to their separate rooms, but both young men were awake for some time, trying to solve what seemed for the moment an unsolvable problem.

*

As they rode down the course, Charles looked at Indira and felt that his heart was behaving in a very strange manner, and he told himself that he had to be careful.

'She is too damned pretty for any man's peace of mind!' he thought. And he knew, because her eyes were shining and her lips smiling, that she looked very different from the frightened, unhappy girl they had rescued from the hands of her father's crooked Solicitor.

When they reached the starting-point, the horses were already beginning to get into place, and several gentlemen came up to speak to Charles and Jimmy, then looked at Indira in a manner which made it very clear that they wished to be introduced.

Because he was sure it was the last thing she wanted, Charles deliberately ignored every hint they made, while Indira, concerned with making a fuss of *Meteor* and talking to him in her own special manner, did not even notice.

Lady Sinclair arrived looking exceedingly lovely and very obviously aware of it.

She was again playing hostess, and she said to be other women riders:

"It is so delightful of you to come and take part. I know you will help me to show the gentlemen riders that we are worthy of being the first competitors the dear Marquis has ever allowed to race in his Steeple-Chase."

"How did you persuade him to let us in?" somebody asked.

Lady Sinclair lowered her eye-lashes and looked coy.

"You must not ask me such embarrassing questions," she

said, "but I can assure you I had to be very, very persuasive."

The innuendo in her words was very obvious, and Indira deliberately moved out of earshot to the other end of the starting-line.

Quite a number of riders were in place before the Marquis came riding up on *Thunderer,* which was the name of his stallion.

He moved in front of them, and the chattering voices died away into silence as it became obvious that he had something to say.

"Now, let me make it quite clear once again," he began. "We all race together over the first five fences, then where the course divides the ladies will take the left-hand fork, where there are five more fences, and will reach what is really the first winning-post."

He paused for a moment, then continued:

"The rest of us go on to where you know the course ends, and I am sure it is unnecessary for me to say that the first person to pass the second winning-post will receive the Ardsley Steeple-Chase Cup and one thousand guineas!"

He saw that one or two of the men look surprised and he added:

"The other thousand guineas will be given to the winning lady, together with an attractive prize which she can place round her neck."

Somebody made a joke about this, and amidst the laughter the Marquis said:

"I suggest you now get into place, and as usual when the flag drops that is the signal for the 'off.'"

As he finished speaking he rode to the left of the starting-line, where Indira was waiting with Charles and Jimmy.

Unlike some of the other horses, *Meteor* was standing quite still, and she had no trouble holding him in, but there was an alertness about him which made her think of the T'ang horse which she had held in her hands yesterday.

Strangely enough, as the Marquis came up to her, she had the feeling that he was thinking the same thing.

"Are you all right?" he asked. "Do not hurry *Meteor* over the first fences, and he will easily carry you ahead for the last five."

"I am sure he will," Indira replied, "and he is looking forward to the race as much as I am."

"I hope . . ." the Marquis began, then hesitated.

Indira knew he was about to say that he hoped she would win, then even as he spoke she was aware that Lady Sinclair had come up behind him.

"I should get into position, Rosie," he said. "Some horses get very obstreperous when kept waiting."

"I am well aware of that, Seldon," Lady Sinclair replied, "but you omitted to wish me luck, and you know I shall not feel lucky without your good wishes . . ."

She paused, then said softly, so that only he could hear what she said:

". . . and your love."

There was a frown between the Marquis's eyes.

He had not missed the way Lady Sinclair had behaved at luncheon, and now he thought that only a very stupid woman would be so indiscreet as to parade her affection for him in public and in such company.

He knew that a number of the County families taking part were very strait-laced and in the past had expressed their disapproval of the Prince Regent and his friends.

While the Marquis was not particular about what was said about him in London, he had always been very careful in the country to protect himself against any hint of scandal.

It was obvious that he was talked about, and he would have been stupid if he had not realised that sooner or later gossip concerning his *affaires de coeur* would be carried almost on the wind from London to Hampshire.

But it usually was a slow process, and by the time Hampshire was discussing some beauty with whom he was said to be infatuated, the whole affair was over and her place had been taken by somebody else.

So when he was at Ardsley Hall the Marquis was careful to see that his parties, rather to the surprise of his friends, did nothing to offend the local hierarchy.

In fact, when he invited any of his more raffish contemporaries to stay, he was very careful not to include any of the local people in his dinner-parties.

As a result, although they undoubtedly talked and were curious as to who was staying with him, it was all hearsay, and they could never actually substantiate what they suspected.

Now he thought angrily that he had made a great mistake in allowing Lady Sinclair to persuade him to let women ride, or even having her as a guest when he was running his Steeple-Chase.

He knew that she was being particularly outrageous for the simple reason that last night he had gone to his own bedroom after saying good-night to her.

Although undoubtedly she would have expected him to come to her room later to make love to her before saying good-night again, he had merely got into his own bed and gone to sleep.

Ever since she had come downstairs this morning she had been trying to inveigle him into being alone with her, and he was quite certain that she was going to ask him what was wrong.

But adroitly he had avoided a *tête-à-tête*, or even a low-voiced conversation, which was what she was seeking.

He knew now from the expression in her eyes and the hard note in her voice that she was growing increasingly angry.

However, there was nothing more she could say at the moment, and the Marquis calmly moved away.

After looking to see that all the riders were at the

starting-point, their horses facing in the right direction, he took his own place in the line, then raised his hand to the starter.

The flag went down and they were off. Indira was careful not to rush the first two fences and to keep *Meteor* firmly under control.

The jumps were easy. Even so, there was one fall and another horse refused, which put those following out of their stride.

Then as they jumped the fourth fence, Lady Sinclair shot ahead and sailed over it in a manner which made it quite obvious that she was now straining every nerve to win the race.

The Marquis thought with satisfaction that once the ten ladies were out of the way, it would make the going very much easier for the men, who would certainly require no distractions if they were to survive the very high fences he had erected over the rest of the course.

He himself always enjoyed a challenge, and although he was aware that he had an advantage in that his horses were superb and he had had the opportunity of practising over this particular course during the past month, he knew too that he had some stiff competition to face.

This was provided by riders who had come not only from Hampshire but from several adjacent Counties merely because they wished to compete against him.

They would do everything in their power to prove their horses superior and their riding as good as his, if not better.

The Marquis thought with satisfaction that if he did win, it would not be an easy victory, and he and *Thunderer* would both have to prove themselves exceptional to keep the Ardsley Cup at the Hall.

He settled down to ride with his usual expertise, which made him seem part of the horse, and he knew as he did so that *Thunderer* was enjoying himself as much as he was, while the other riders were straining and urging their mounts at the first all-male fence.

It was high and certainly formidable, but without exception each horse swept over it, landing without mishap to go on to the next jump.

It was after they had jumped the third fence that the Marquis glanced to his left and thought he must be mistaken.

Then he saw to his astonishment that while the other nine ladies had obeyed his instructions and left the course where he had told them to do so, Indira was still riding with the men and was a little ahead of the field.

"Why the hell could she not have done as she was told?" the Marquis asked himself angrily.

Then as he took the next fence with perfect timing and realised that she had done the same, he thought with a twist of his lips how angry Rosie Sinclair would be and that no other woman he knew would have dared to jump this part of the course as he had laid it out.

Then as he jumped the next fence he heard just behind him a horse fall, and he had a sudden fear that Indira might fall too.

She looked so frail and so graceful mounted on *Meteor* that he could not bear to think of her being thrown to the ground and perhaps injured.

He wondered if he could reach her and order her to pull out of the race, then knew it would be impossible and there was nothing he could do but ride on and hope that by some miracle she would survive.

The next two fences were particularly difficult, and as one rider after another cleared them, the Marquis felt even as *Thunderer* leapt over them that he was willing Indira to clear them too.

Now the field was thinning out considerably. At the same time, riderless horses, which were always a danger, had struggled to their feet and were galloping on regardless of the fact that there was no-one on their backs.

One of them crossed in front of a rider, and he let out a stream of oaths before his horse stumbled on landing and threw him over its head.

When there were only two fences left, the Marquis was aware that there were five riders clear of the rest. Indira was level with *Thunderer*, and only about two lengths behind were Charles, Jimmy, and Lord Neville.

As Lord Neville was on one of the Marquis's finest horses, it was not surprising that he was one of the leaders.

The Marquis knew that although he was a good rider, he was not exceptional, and at the next fence, a very difficult one, he lost nearly a length.

After the last fence the Marquis had arranged that there was a long stretch of flat ground before the winning-post, and it was on this run-in that he knew the best horses would show both their stamina and their speed.

Somehow it was not a surprise when he found himself racing neck-and-neck with Indira.

It was what he might have expected, he thought, and yet at the same time he had never envisaged that his closest competitor for the trophy he had won four years in succession would be a woman.

It was then that he realised what was giving Indira her advantage. *Thunderer* was indeed a slightly better horse than *Meteor*, but he was also carrying a far greater weight.

As they started to race over the flat ground, the Marquis knew unmistakably that this year he had met his match, and he would not win the Cup as he had so confidently expected.

Then as the winning-post came in sight, he was aware, to his surprise, that he was gaining, and *Thunderer* was now a few inches ahead of *Meteor*.

For a moment he thought he must be mistaken, but when he looked again he knew it was the truth.

She was not urging her horse on, as anybody would have expected, but instead was using all her strength to hold him back.

It was so surprising that the Marquis could hardly ask himself why she should do such a thing, before they had passed the winning-post amidst roars of applause, and he was aware that he and *Thunderer* had won the Steeple-Chase by a head.

He rode on a little way until he could draw *Thunderer* in, and Indira did the same.

As the horses slowed down to a walk, he turned to her and said:

"I can hardly believe that any woman could complete such a course, and I should be very angry with you for risking your neck."

"You . . . should be . . . congratulating . . . *Meteor*," Indira said breathlessly. "He flew over the . . . fences and never put a . . . foot wrong."

"All the same, it was a risk you should not have taken," the Marquis said severely.

She smiled at him and he knew that she was as excited as any other rider would have been.

Then as Charles and Jimmy came galloping towards them, followed by Lord Neville and several other riders, he said quietly:

"I want an explanation as to why you pulled in *Meteor* on the run-in, for I am well aware that you could have beaten me."

He saw the colour come into her face, but before she was forced to reply, Charles had joined them.

"How can—you have done—anything so—crazy?" he asked, his breath coming in gasps between his lips.

"His Lordship was just asking the same question," Indira replied.

"You were wonderful!" Jimmy cried as he joined them. "I

would never have believed that any woman could ride like that."

"And no woman shall again," the Marquis said sharply. "I will not allow them to compete another year."

"That is not fair!" Indira cried. "And it would make me miserable to think I had excluded others from this wonderful race."

"We know only too well what you think about women, Ardsley," Charles said with a laugh, "but you must admit that Indira has confounded you and upset all your theories."

The Marquis was saved from answering by Lord Neville, and several other riders who came up, all conveying to Indira their astonishment that she had finished the course.

Then as she blushed and looked a little embarrassed, they reached the crowds of spectators and there were loud cheers and men waving their hands.

At the winning-post itself, Indira saw the other women competitors grouped behind it, and Lady Sinclair was looking at her with an expression of undisguised fury on her face.

Instinctively she tightened her hands on the reins, and as *Meteor* slowed down so that the horsemen riding beside her moved ahead, she looked away from Lady Sinclair, wondering what she should say and if she should apologise to the Marquis for embarrassing him.

Then she saw another face and gave a little gasp of sheer horror.

Standing in the crowd watching her approach was Mr. Jacobson!

For a moment Indira felt as if she could not think and her head was filled with cotton-wool.

Then as if it were the only action open to her, she turned *Meteor,* and before anybody, including Charles, who was beside her, realised what she was about to do, she rode off

the course and behind the coaches onto the open meadowland.

There she touched *Meteor* with her whip, and without
looking back she galloped straight for the house.

When she arrived, Indira dismounted at the front door
and a groom came running to *Meteor*'s head.

"'Ow did yer get on, Miss?" he asked.

"*Meteor* came in second," Indira replied.

The groom looked dejected.

"Oi lost me money! Oi was certain ye'd be first."

Because he sounded so disappointed, Indira said:

"I came second in the main race to His Lordship and
Thunderer!"

The man gaped at her as she walked away and up the
steps into the Hall.

She went to her bedroom, and when the maids came to
help her she took off her habit and changed into an
afternoon-gown. At the same time, she was wondering what
she should do.

Mr. Jacobson had found her, and she was thankful that
Charles and Jimmy were there to protect her. But she was
quite sure he would make trouble, although what form that
would take she had no idea.

He could not forcibly drag her to London to marry Lord
Bredon if they objected. At the same time, she really had no
claim on them, although she was sure they would do everything to protect her.

"You must help me, Papa," she said to her father as she
stared in the mirror without seeing her reflection or even
being aware that the maid was arranging her hair.

In her mind she spoke to her father, as she had spoken to
him last night, without fear.

Instead she felt a calmness that she had not known before, and the terror that Mr. Jacobson had invoked in her
when he had first revealed his plan of marrying her to the
fortune-hunter had gone.

She knew it was because in some strange, unaccountable way the Marquis had dispelled her terror and unhappiness and had given her a confidence that she had lost from the moment her father had died so suddenly and tragically.

Now Indira was certain he was guiding and protecting her and nothing terrible could happen that she would not be able to cope with once he told her what to do.

Because she was sure that the Marquis's guests would all be coming back to the house to celebrate his victory, she did not go downstairs.

When the maids had left her she sat in her bedroom, thinking of her father and sending out her thoughts towards him so that she could somehow link herself with him.

She had been extremely interested in thought-transference when she was in India, but it was something she had never needed to practise because her father had always been with her.

Now she felt as if the vibrations within herself were seeking his. At the same time, although she found it hard to understand, she felt as if she also vibrated towards the Marquis, and because he was in the same world as she was he would be aware of it.

"I am being ridiculous," she told herself. "He will only be thinking of Lady Sinclair, not of me. But because he . . . understood as no-one else except Papa has ever done . . . I know that I . . . need him."

She must have been in her bedroom for nearly an hour when there was a knock on the door, and when she opened it there was a footman outside.

"Excuse me, Miss, but Lord Frodham wants to speak to you, if it's convenient."

"Yes, of course," Indira replied, "Where is His Lordship?"

"His Lordship told me to tell you, My Lady, he'd be in the Study."

"Thank you," Indira said.

She thought that if Charles wanted to speak to her secretly, it was certainly astute of him to realise that the Marquis would not allow crowds of guests to invade a room which, she was aware, as Charles was, was essentially his own.

She hurried down the stairs, wondering if Charles had seen Mr. Jacobson as she had, and what he and Jimmy would feel about it.

It was impossible to speculate on what they would say or what they would do, but she was not as terror-struck as she knew she would have been yesterday.

A footman opened the door of the Study and she went inside to find both Charles and Jimmy.

She thought they were looking very serious, but as she walked across the room towards them Jimmy said:

"You were magnificent! There is no other word for it! You had everybody who came to watch the race absolutely astounded!"

Indira smiled at him a little shyly before Charles said:

"There is something much more important to talk about at the moment."

"Mr. Jacobson!" Indira said in a low voice.

"Exactly," Charles answered. "I suspected you had seen him and that was why you rode away."

"I thought it was the . . . best thing to . . . do."

"You were right!" Jimmy exclaimed. "And you missed Lady Sinclair throwing a tantrum and screaming at the Marquis."

"What about?"

"About you, of course! She accused him of deliberately sending her and the other ladies on a different course so that you could win the race with him."

"She made a fool of herself," Charles said briefly, "but we have to tell Indira what else has happened."

"What is it?"

Charles drew some papers out of the pocket of his riding-coat.

"Jacobson handed me these," he said, "and quite frankly I do not know what I am going to do about them."

"What are they?" Indira asked.

"One is a writ which orders me to go in front of the Magistrates to explain why I abducted a minor," Charles replied, "and the other accuses Jimmy and me of inflicting grevious bodily harm upon a Solicitor who was merely carrying out his orders."

For a moment Indira stared at him as if she could not credit what he had said.

Then she gave a cry of horror before she exclaimed:

"Can he really bring these charges against you? And if he does, what will . . . happen?"

Chapter Six

THERE was silence, as both young men considered the question. Then Jimmy said:

"I think, frankly, he is trying to blackmail us. He knows that we will not want a scandal and thinks we will pay to keep him quiet."

"If he brings charges," Charles replied harshly, "he will put a noose round his own neck. After all, there is Indira's evidence that he was trying to force her into marriage so that he could get hold of her money."

Even as he spoke he knew that the publicity such a case would create might destroy Jacobson, but it would also damage Indira's reputation so that no hostess in any strata of Society would accept her as a guest.

Indira clasped her hands together.

"I am sorry . . . so terribly sorry," she said, "that I have . . . involved you in . . . this."

"You could not help it," Charles replied, "and somehow we will give that cheating devil his just dues. I only wish I had hit him harder!"

"It was hard enough for him to bring a charge against you," Jimmy said.

Charles gave a sharp laugh.

"You do not suppose that would stand up in Court?"

Jimmy knew that was true.

Charles was a Nobleman, and it would be acknowledged that he was absolutely justified in dealing as he had with a man like Jacobson, considering that he had been physically menacing a woman.

At the same time, this once again involved Indira, and both Charles and Jimmy knew that somehow they had to keep her out of the mess.

"I refuse to buy him off," Charles said suddenly and violently, "and before we return to London on Monday we have to think of a way of making that clear to him."

"It might be a good idea to go and see the Lord Chief Justice," Jimmy said. "He is a friend of my father's, although I have never met him personally."

"Whatever we do, we have to think it out very carefully," Charles replied, "in order to save Indira from being involved."

"But I am involved," Indira said, "and it is very sweet of you to think of me. At the same time, I am only a . . . stranger and have no . . . right to . . . impose upon you."

Charles looked at her and wondered what she would say if he told her she meant very much more to him than a stranger would.

Then he told himself it was too soon to say anything like that, and in any case how could he ask her to marry him, seeing what his family would say about it and how unhappy they would undoubtedly make her?

With an effort he said calmly:

"This is no time for us to make decisions, and we can talk tomorrow when it will be easier than it is now."

He glanced at the door as he spoke, almost as if he expected the Marquis to come in.

"You are right," Jimmy said, "the house is full of people celebrating our host's victory, and there is to be a large dinner-party which the Marquis always gives after the Steeple-Chase."

"If there is to be a dinner-party to celebrate his victory, and if Lady Sinclair is a winner too," Indira said, "I think it would be wise for me to stay upstairs."

As she spoke she thought that Charles was about to pro-
test, and she added quickly:

"As a matter of fact, I do feel rather tired."

"That is not surprising," Jimmy said. "I am tired too, and
I never believed any woman could complete that very
difficult course as splendidly as you did."

"You really have to thank *Meteor* for that," Indira said
with a smile. "At the same time, it would be a mistake for
people to . . . praise me when Lady Sinclair is . . . there."

Both men knew that she was nervous as to what Lady
Sinclair might say to her or how she would behave.

Seeing the way Her Ladyship had raged at the Marquis
and shocked quite a number of his friends, neither Charles
nor Jimmy wished for her to be so rude and aggressive to
Indira.

"You are quite sure that is what you want to do?" Jimmy
asked.

"I am quite sure!" Indira said firmly. "I will send a message to His Lordship to say that I have retired to bed and
hope he will excuse me."

Charles nodded as if he thought that was right. Then he
added:

"I think you should disappear now, otherwise if the Marquis knows you are downstairs, he might suspect you have
reasons other than tiredness for not appearing at dinner."

"Yes, of course," Indira agreed. "And I will go up to my
room by a side staircase. Good-night, Charles."

She would have left, but Charles took her hand in his and
said:

"I cannot let you go without telling you how wonderful
you were! I was terrified when I first realised you were
jumping the higher fences with us. Then I just prayed you
would complete the course and confound them all."

"Especially Lady Sinclair!" Jimmy added. "I have never

seen a more disgraceful exhibition than she made of herself. It was worthy of a Billingsgate fish-wife!"

Charles did not appear to hear him. He was just looking
at Indira, until he said in a deep voice:

"We will talk about it all tomorrow. Good-night, Indira,
and do not worry. Jimmy and I will look after you."

"Thank you."

He hesitated but did not release her hand.

Then as she looked at him enquiringly he raised it a little
awkwardly to his lips.

"The Marquis should give you a special prize for brav-
ery," he said, "and I would like to do the same."

Indira did not blush or seem embarrassed. She merely
took her hand from his, smiled at him, then at Jimmy, and
slipped out of the room.

Charles glanced at the door after she had left, almost as if
he considered following her.

"No-one could be more sensible," Jimmy said. "It would
have been disastrous for her to come down to dinner and
have Lady Sinclair making snide remarks all the evening, if
not being openly rude."

"One thing is quite certain," Charles said, "Lady Sinclair
has cooked her goose where the Marquis is concerned. I was
watching his face when she was raging at him, and he
looked not only more contemptuous than usual but positively disgusted!"

"I was disgusted too," Jimmy said, "and if that is the way
in which women with 'blue blood' behave, then all I can say
is give me a tradesman's daughter every time."

"I agree with you," Charles answered. "At the same time,
I cannot believe most tradesmen's daughters are like Indira."

"I can still hardly believe that she was within an inch of
beating the Marquis," Jimmy enthused.

"Well, she was, and what we have to decide now," Charles said, "is what we are going to do about Jacobson."

"If we had had any sense," Jimmy replied, "we should have drowned him when we had the chance!"

*

Indira reached her bedroom without seeing anybody and crossed the room for a moment to look out at the sun sinking behind the oak trees in the Park. It turned not only the sky but also the lake to crimson and gold.

It was so lovely that she felt as if her whole being reached out to the beauty of it, but she knew that she had to say good-bye.

"Help me, Papa, help me!" she prayed in her heart. "I cannot let these two young men who have been so kind get into trouble because of me. I need all your cleverness and power of organisation to help me at this moment."

Almost as if her prayer had brought her an answer, she walked across the room to tug at the bell-pull which was a strip of exquisitely embroidered satin hanging down from the ceiling.

She went back to the window and waited until there was a knock at the door and the maid who usually attended her came it.

"You rang, M'Lady?"

"Yes, Emily. I wonder if you would be so kind as to ask the Housekeeper to come here as soon as she can."

"I'll fetch Mrs. Baker right away, M'Lady. She's not far away."

The maid left the room, and Indira waited only a few minutes before Mrs. Baker, an elderly woman with white hair, and dressed in rustling black silk with a silver *chatelaine* at her waist, came into the room.

"You wished to see me, M'Lady?" she asked, shutting the door behind her.

"Yes, Mrs. Baker," Indira replied. "I need your help."

"Of course, M'Lady, I'll do anything I can."

"When I returned from the Steeple-Chase," Indira began, "I received a message to say that somebody very close and dear to me had died."

"I'm sorry to hear that, M'Lady."

"You will understand, Mrs. Baker, that I have to leave immediately for London, but I have no wish to upset or cast an atmosphere of gloom over His Lordship's victory-party."

"I can understand that, M'Lady."

"That is why I need your assistance," Indira went on, "and only with your help can I leave immediately without anybody being aware of it."

"Immediately, M'Lady?"

Indira nodded.

"I am needed in London as quickly as I can get there. But it is not going to be easy, because I was brought here by Lord Frodham and Sir James Overton, who had agreed to take me on Monday to some relatives who live about fifteen miles away."

Mrs. Baker was listening attentively as Indira continued:

"Now that my plans have changed, I must somehow get to London, and you can understand I would not wish to spoil their stay here at Ardsley Hall or to disrupt His Lordship's arrangements for dinner."

"I do see it's a problem, M'Lady."

"What I was going to suggest," Indira said, "if you could possibly arrange it, was to have a carriage to take me to the nearest Posting-Inn, where after a short night's rest I can hire some horses to take me on to London first thing tomorrow morning."

Mrs. Baker held up her hands in horror.

"Oh, M'Lady, you couldn't do that, and certainly not travel alone!"

"It seems too much to ask," Indira said, "but could one of the maids . . . accompany me?"

"Of course that can be arranged," Mrs. Baker agreed. "It will leave me short-handed when the house's so full, but death, M'Lady, is something none of us can anticipate or arrange to happen at our convenience."

"That is true," Indira murmured.

"What's more," Mrs. Baker went on, her voice warming as she thought out what was required, "I'm sure His Lordship would not wish you to travel in the type of carriage and behind the inferior horses which is all you'll be able to hire at a Posting-Inn."

She paused before she said:

"I'll take it upon myself to see that a carriage takes you to where Your Ladyship'll be staying in London, and of course His Lordship's own horses are stabled along the route so you'll get there very much quicker than you would in a hired carriage."

"Of course you are right," Indira agreed.

"We all have to put our best foot forward, M'Lady, in an emergency."

"I am very, very grateful, and please, will you make quite sure that nobody realises I have left until tomorrow, when I shall be already on my way to London? I will write a note to His Lordship and to Lord Frodham. I know they will understand the circumstances which make me wish to leave at once."

"I think that's very considerate of you, M'Lady," Mrs. Baker said. "There're far too many of those who don't think of other people and are only too ready to inflict their own sufferings upon them."

Without saying any more Mrs. Baker left the room, and a few minutes later Emily and another housemaid came in to start packing Indira's clothes into the three trunks she had brought with her.

She was sitting at the *secretaire* which stood in a corner of her bedroom, and it took her a little time to write two notes, for she had to be very careful what she said.

She was determined to save both Charles and Jimmy from any repercussions arising from their plot to bring her to Ardsley Hall, for she knew, now that she had seen him, that the Marquis was not a man who would tolerate being made a fool of or deceived.

It struck her that it had been very stupid of Charles and Jimmy to have attempted such a thing in the first place, seeing how much they enjoyed taking part in his Steeple-Chase.

Then with a little smile she thought that if they were really her brothers they were behaving exactly as she would have expected, being young enough to think their plot was fun, without really counting the consequences.

She thought very carefully what she would say, and once again had the idea that her father was guiding her hand as she wrote:

My Lord,

It is difficult for me to tell You how much I have enjoyed Your Hospitality and what a Joy and Delight it has been to ride "Meteor."

I am only ashamed that I deceived Lord Frodham and Sir James, when after they so valiantly rescued me I informed them that my Name was Lady Mary Combe.

This is not true, and my only Excuse is that when they suggested, because there seemed to be no alternative, bringing me to Ardsley Hall, I expected to feel over-awed by Your Lordship and the Company in which I would find myself. I therefore was presumptuous enough not to wish to be seen at a disadvantage. I hope You will understand, and Forgive me.

I learnt after the race was over that Somebody very close and dear to me has died, and I therefore have to leave for London immediately.

I have no wish to disrupt, and perhaps cast a gloom over, the Celebrations Your Lordship has planned with such care, and which I know everybody will enjoy.

It may seem exceedingly impertinent to borrow Your carriage, Your horses, and one of your housemaids, but there really was no other alternative, and once again, I can only beg Your forgiveness, and thank You from the bottom of my Heart.

I shall never forget the Days I have spent at Ardsley Hall and seeing your T'ang horse, who will, I know, be often in my Dreams.

Thank you, thank you, My Lord, and please forgive me.

I remain, yours gratefully,
    and penitently,
        Indira Rowlandson.

As she finished the letter, Indira read it through and decided that although there were things she might have added or subtracted, there was really no time to write any more.

Quickly she wrote another letter:

Dear Charles and Jimmy,

I enclose a letter for the Marquis, which I think will explain the whole Position without involving either of you.

I can never thank You both enough for being so kind, helpful, and protective towards me. I cannot bear to think of what might have Happened to me if You had not brought me Here. Now you must not be involved any more in my Affairs, and I know that I can manage them myself. Once I get to London I will find people who knew Papa to help me.

Please do not try to find me, and if Mr. Jacobson approaches you, deny all knowledge of where I have gone, but merely say that you do not expect ever to see me again. I think in those Circumstances that his Writs, if that is what they are, will be useless and if what he really wants is Money he will be unable to obtain it if he cannot find me.

Thank You both for being so kind and protective when I

*needed it most, and I shall think about you with Gratitude for
the rest of my Life.*

I remain forever in your Debt,

Indira

Indira folded the letter she had written to the Marquis,
left it unsealed, and, having written his name on it, placed it
with the one for Charles and Jimmy in an envelope large
enough to hold them both.

She then addressed it to Charles and left it on the *secretaire,* and hurriedly changed into her travelling-gown and
cloak.

By this time the sun had sunk, but she knew there would
still be enough light for her to drive some miles from
Ardsley Hall before it was dark.

She was just tying the ribbons of her bonnet under her
chin when Mrs. Baker came hurrying back into the room.

"Everything's arranged, M'Lady," she said. "I've sent a
message to His Lordship to say you're tired after the race
and won't be joining his guests at dinner, and the carriage is
waiting at a side-door."

"Thank you, Mrs. Baker, you are so very kind," Indira
said.

"I've arranged for Johnson to go with you, M'Lady. She's
one of our oldest housemaids and is used to travelling. She's
waiting downstairs, M'Lady, and there are two footmen
outside ready to take down Your Ladyship's luggage."

At Mrs. Baker's command the two men came into the
bedroom, picked up the trunks which the housemaids had
just finished strapping down, and carried them away.

Indira gave the two maids such a large tip that they were
almost incoherent with gratitude, curtseying to her several
times, before escorted by Mrs. Baker she went along the
corridors of the house and down a staircase which led to the
side-door.

Here waiting for her was an elderly maid correctly dressed in a black bonnet and shawl.

"This is Johnson, M'Lady," Mrs. Baker said. "She'll look after you for as long as you want her, then she'll return here with the carriage."

Indira put out her hand to thank Mrs. Baker, who said:

"You are too young and too pretty, M'Lady, to suffer, and I'll be thinking of you and praying that all'll go well for you in the future."

The way she spoke Indira found very moving, and she answered:

"Thank you, Mrs. Baker, and it is not only His Lordship who has made me very welcome since I came to Ardsley Hall, but all of you who have looked after me and been so kind."

She then went through the door and out to where the carriage was waiting.

It was a closed barouche drawn by two horses, and there were a coachman and a footman on the box. As she waved good-bye to Mrs. Baker, she thought how lucky she was to be travelling in such comfort rather than in the inferior type of vehicle she would have to hire at a Posting-Inn.

As they went down the drive and she turned to look back at the house, she felt as if a chapter in her life was closing and she was leaving something which strangely meant a great deal to her, to set off once again into the unknown.

The lights in the windows of the great house glowed golden in the fading light, and involuntarily her thoughts went to the T'ang horse in the Library.

The horse, she thought, had changed her whole attitude towards life, and she felt a sharp pang of regret and an even deeper emotion that she must leave in such a furtive manner.

Then she knew almost as if somebody were telling her so that it was not only the horse she minded leaving but its owner, the Marquis.

He had been her guide, her Guru, and had directed her back to the right path, which she should never have left in the first place.

There was so much more she wanted to learn from him, so much she felt he could tell her, and yet because Charles and James must not be hurt by Mr. Jacobson, she had to leave him without even saying good-bye.

The horses had passed under the oak trees which bordered the drive, and now the house was gradually being obscured by their branches.

Ahead were the massive gold-tipped gates with their attendant lodges and she knew that in a few seconds more the house would be lost to her sight forever.

Then, without her conscious volition, her heart said:

"Good-bye, my guide, my Master, and my love!"

Incredibly, she was aware that she was speaking to the Marquis.

*

Indira arrived in London on Tuesday morning about noon.

It had been a long journey but a comfortable one, because the Marquis's coachman did not hurry his horses but drove them smoothly and with great care.

Indira stayed three nights at the best Posting-Inns on the way, and as she was travelling with the Marquis's servants she was received with great respect, and was automatically given a bedroom with a room next door for her maid, and a private Parlour.

Because she had no wish to be alone, Johnson had supper with her and proved to be a most interesting source of information about Ardsley Hall and the distinguished guests who were entertained there.

"Forty-five years I've been at the Hall, M'Lady," Johnson said in her prim voice, "and I've seen many changes, and not all of them for the better. But I can honestly say that it's a happy house, and we're very proud of it."

Because Indira was genuinely interested in what the maid had to say, she drew her out and thought when she went up to bed that she had not really missed being at the Marquis's dinner-party.

On Sunday night it was difficult to concentrate on what Johnson was saying, because she kept wondering what Charles and Jimmy had thought when they learnt she had disappeared, and whether the Marquis himself was glad to be rid of her.

She knew it was really her fault that Lady Sinclair had lost her temper and raged at him, and she felt too that he would be annoyed to learn that she had deceived him by giving a false name and pretending to be a titled Lady.

"It is the sort of behaviour he despises utterly!" she told herself.

She hoped that Charles and Jimmy would not be so foolish as to reveal that they were aware of her true identity.

If they did so, it would completely destroy her plan to save them not only from Mr. Jacobson but also from offending the Marquis.

"I am sure, Papa," she said to her father in the darkness, "that I have done the only sporting thing I can do and that you approve. At the same time, I would like to have stayed at Ardsley Hall a little longer and had another talk with the Marquis."

It was not really until Sunday night that she admitted to herself that what she felt for him was very different from anything she had ever felt for any other man.

She had often talked to her father about falling in love, and he had said to her:

"You must not be in a hurry, my darling. As you are very beautiful as well as rich, there will be dozens, if not hundreds, of men who will lay their hearts at your feet, but I am determined to make quite sure that the man you marry is somebody who loves you for yourself—the real you, whom I know and adore."

Thinking back, Indira understood exactly what her father had meant, for until now she had never been alone
with a man and there had been no question of flirtations or
of anyone making love to her.

Because they were travelling about so much, this was
understandable, and also since the parties they had attended were always given for her father, Indira was usually
the youngest person present.

She had known that one of his reasons for coming to
England was that he wanted her to lead a more social life
than they had managed to do in the East, and to meet what
he sometimes called "the right type of men."

"What do you mean by that, Papa?" she had asked once.

"You will know what I mean when you meet one," he
replied.

She knew now he would have approved of the Marquis,
who was a Gentleman in every sense of the word.

He was also a magnificent rider and sportsman, and,
unexpectedly—yet of course it must be attributed to
fate—he was somebody who had understood what the
T'ang horse had meant to her, and the Chinese verses that
had been written centuries ago.

"I found him, Papa," she said in her heart, "but I have . . .
lost him . . . again. And now I understand what you were
talking about."

But to understand did not alleviate the strange pain that
she felt in her heart when she thought about the Marquis,
and an irrepressible longing to go to him with her troubles
and beg for his help.

She knew he would have understood the problems of
arriving alone in England without her father, and that he
would have dealt very effectively with the traitor Jacobson.
At the same time, she was also sure that the Marquis would
expect them to find her relatives.

"It cannot be so difficult if I think about it," she told
herself.

When she awoke early on Tuesday morning, she had the

feeling that once again her father was directing her in doing what was right.

Having breakfasted, she and Johnson went into the yard of the Posting-Inn, where the carriage was waiting for them.

The footman, as he handed Indira into it, asked:

"Where would you wish me to take you, M'Lady, when we reach London?"

As if her father prompted her, Indira gave him the answer.

*

Early on Monday morning the Marquis had said good-bye to the last of his guests, and as they drove away in Phaetons, travelling Chariots, and Chaises, he walked swiftly across the Hall towards his Study.

He entered it to find Charles and Jimmy waiting for him, both of them looking slightly apprehensive.

"I asked you to wait," the Marquis said without preamble, "until my other guests had departed, so that I could talk to you about Lady Mary, or shall we call her Indira Rowlandson?"

The way he spoke without innuendo in his voice brought a feeling of relief to the young men listening to him.

The Marquis walked to stand with his back to the mantelpiece as he said:

"Suppose you sit down and tell me where she has gone?"

"I am afraid we have no idea," Charles replied.

There was a frown between the Marquis's eyes as he said:

"Are you telling me that she did not give you an address?"

"No."

"But surely you must have some idea which relative has died and caused her to leave in that precipitate manner?"

"I am afraid the answer is again 'No,'" Jimmy said before Charles could speak. "In fact, when we saw her after the race, she did not mention that she was thinking of leaving. She said that we could talk the next day and decide where she should go when we took her to London."

"So that was what you intended to do?" the Marquis asked.

Charles said quickly:

"She had talked of going to some people who live not far away in the country, but I gathered that since she had been here she had changed her mind."

It sounded a little lame, but the Marquis merely said:

"Well, perhaps my Coachman will be able to enlighten us further, but if for the moment you are as ignorant about her arrangements as I am, then there is nothing further to discuss."

"No, nothing," Charles agreed firmly, "but as Jimmy and I are going to London, we will certainly see if we can find her."

The Marquis did not reply, and rising to his feet Charles said a little diffidently:

"I am sorry, My Lord, that you should have been deceived in any way."

"I suppose you have never heard of Miss Rowlandson's father?"

"Rowlandson is quite a common name," Charles replied. "I do not expect he is any relation of the Cartoonist."

As Jimmy thought that any further probing on the part of the Marquis might be dangerous, he interposed to say:

"I think we should be starting for London, My Lord, and if we do hear anything about Indira's whereabouts, we will of course, if you are interested, let you know."

"You can leave a message for me at White's," the Marquis said sharply.

They said good-bye and thanked him for the Steeple-Chase and for entertaining them so well, but they both thought as they spoke that the Marquis was not really attending to what they were saying, but seemed to be preoccupied by his own thoughts.

Only when they were driving off in Charles's Phaeton did Jimmy say:

"Indira certainly got us out of that difficulty very cleverly, but what are we going to do about Jacobson?"

"Nothing," Charles said. "She is right, and I have the feeling he will not make a scene at Ardsley Hall, although he may try to get in touch with us in London."

"How do you think he found us in the first place?"

Before Charles could answer, he exclaimed:

"But of course! You gave your name to the Inn-Keeper. I thought at the time it was unnecessary."

"That is easy for you to say now," Charles replied. "But you know as well as I do that if he had thought us ordinary travellers he would not have produced his best brandy, which you were only too delighted to pour down your throat!"

Jimmy laughed.

"Well, another time you should travel incognito. I can see only too clearly what happened. Jacobson learnt who we were and that we had taken Indira with us. Your groom would have boasted in the stables where we were going. And we were near enough to the Hall to have everybody talking about the Steeple-Chase."

"You are certainly making some good deductions about what occurred in the past," Charles remarked, "but that does not bring us any nearer to finding Indira in the future."

"Do you intend to find her?" Jimmy asked.

"Of course I intend to find her. You know as well as I do that she can no more look after herself than can a babe in arms."

"All the same," Jimmy expostulated, "it was very clever of her to take the Marquis's carriage to London, and one of the maids as a Chaperone to look after her."

"How did you find out all that?" Charles asked curiously.

"I asked the Butler and the Housekeeper. I suspect there had already been enquiries by the Marquis as to how she had left."

"I think she might have told us what she was doing," Charles complained.

"If you think about it logically," Jimmy said, "you will realise that she was thinking of you and me and saving us from being mixed up with Jacobson."

"Yes, that is true," Charles agreed, "and there are very few women who would be so unselfish."

Before Jimmy could speak he added:

"But dammit! I wish she had trusted me! I fear she will get into a lot of trouble if she is on her own, and we will not be there to save her."

*

The Marquis, as it happened, was thinking very much the same thing.

Now that he knew Indira was not Lady Mary Combe as she had pretended to be, it made him even more apprehensive about her than he would have been otherwise.

Although, as Lord Wrotham had said, she certainly did not look as if she had come from India, he was astute enough to realise that there were many things in England that were strange to her, and that what he accepted as a matter of course, she regarded with curiosity.

'She is so young and so lovely,' he thought, 'It is impossible for her to be on her own.'

He wished now he had questioned Charles and Jimmy far more closely than he had, but he had felt slightly uncomfortable about revealing how very interested he was in Indira.

He also suspected that part of what they had told him had been untrue, although he had no logical reason for thinking so.

What had worried him ever since her arrival seemed now to grow more complicated and more puzzling, so that he went over every conversation he had had with her, and at the end of it was only more bewildered than he had been at the beginning.

It seemed extraordinary that anyone as lovely and as expensively gowned as Indira should be travelling alone, and having appeared from nowhere had vanished into nowhere without his being able to do anything about it.

As he had every intention of finding her, the Marquis concentrated his thoughts on her all the time he was travelling to London.

He had perfected a means of travelling with great speed when it was necessary.

He left the Hall, driving himself in a light Phaeton with six horses. Only a Corinthian with his expertise could have managed such a large team on the main roads and driven until it was dark at a record pace.

He then had an excellent dinner which had been provided by his own Chef at a Posting-Inn, and when he finished, a closed travelling Chariot drawn by a team of four was waiting for him.

Driven by his most experienced Coachman all through the night—fortunately there was a moon—the Marquis slept peacefully until dawn.

After a bath and breakfast he set off again, driving another Phaeton with four perfectly matched horses, which reached London by one o'clock.

At Ardsley House in Park Lane, the Marquis changed his clothes before setting out again, in another Phaeton and with fresh horses, for Whitehall.

He was not feeling tired after the long hours of driving and admitted to himself that the reason for his haste could be expressed in one word—Indira.

The Marquis had always tried to be honest with himself and his feelings.

In fact, he had always known that he despised quite enough of what he found in the world about him and was therefore scrupulously frank when he faced his own emotions about anything or anybody.

Now he admitted, although with reluctance, that his

search for Indira was serious to the point where not only his brain was involved but also his heart.

He supposed that he had really fallen in love with her when he had seen her come into the Drawing-Room accompanied by Charles and Jimmy and thought she was the most beautiful girl he had ever seen in his whole life.

Then when he talked to her he had found her so refreshingly different from what he had expected, but he had also been aware that she was in fear of something.

He had been intrigued to the point where he had found it hard to be aware of the existence of any other women in the room.

He had known when his feelings for Lady Sinclair had altered so suddenly and completely that there must be some reason for it. At the same time, it was something he did not wish to put into words, even though his instinct said it for him.

Now that he had lost Indira and she had vanished in that unexpected and unaccountable manner, he knew he had to find her again.

When after breakfast on Sunday morning he read the letter she had written to him, his impulse had been to rage at everybody in the house for not having informed him that one of his guests had left so suddenly.

But because he had exceptional self-control, when he sent for Mrs. Baker he had appeared to accept with approval the arrangements she had made when Indira had told her she must go to London.

"Her Ladyship was thinking of Your Lordship," Mrs. Baker said, "and I said to her it was very considerate, and many ladies'd want sympathy and condolences, and would be thinking of no-one but themselves."

She thought the Marquis looked approving and went on:

"Although I were worried, M'Lord, that anyone so young and so beautiful should go off alone in such a manner, there was nothing I could do but send Johnson with Her Lady-

ship, and I asked for one of Your Lordship's most reliable
and ablest Coachmen, knowing he would see there was no
trouble on the journey."

"That was very sensible of you, Mrs. Baker," the Marquis
said. "But Her Ladyship did not tell you exactly where she
was staying in London?"

"No, Your Lordship. But the Coachman'll know where
when he gets back."

"Yes, of course," the Marquis agreed.

He knew that having deposited Indira he would have
taken the horses to the stables behind Ardsley House.

As he was changing his clothes he sent a footman to the
Mews, and when he came downstairs it was to find Jackson,
a middle-aged man who was an excellent driver, waiting for
him in the Hall.

"Good-afternoon, Jackson."

"Art'noon, M'Lord."

"Did you have a good journey up from the country?"

"Aye, M'Lord, very good. We've just arrived, and them
new bays be shapin' up well."

"I am glad to hear it," the Marquis answered. "Her Ladyship was not upset by the journey?"

"Nay, M'Lord."

There was a little pause before the Marquis asked:

"Where did you put Her Ladyship down, Jackson?"

"It so 'appens, M'Lord, that Her Ladyship asks me to
leave her at some Livery Stables on the outskirts o' London."

The Marquis stared at Jackson in astonishment. Then he
asked:

"What was the reason for that?"

"Oi've no idea, M'Lord. 'Cept that's wot 'Er Ladyship
asks."

"And when you left her there did you just drive away?"

"Aye, M'Lord."

The Marquis did not speak, and after a moment the
Coachman said:

"Oi 'opes I done right, M'Lord, Oi only done wot 'Er Ladyship asks."

"Yes, yes, that was quite right."

The Marquis walked to the front door and outside to where his Phaeton was waiting.

As he climbed into it he thought despairingly that Indira was determined to cover her tracks and that it was going to be more difficult than he had expected to find her again.

However, he drove to the Colonial Office and asked to see Earl Bathurst, who agreed to see him immediately.

The Marquis was aware that the various territories acquired by the British over generations were administered partly by the Secretaries of State for War and for the Colonies, and partly by great Chartered Companies.

The Earl, who was the Colonial Secretary of State, rose at his entrance and said:

"I am surprised to see you, Ardsley. I thought you were in the country."

"I have just come back to London," the Marquis replied, "and I have one or two questions I would like to ask you."

Earl Bathurst smiled jovially and settled himself comfortably in his armchair.

"Ask away," he said.

"First," the Marquis said, "is the Earl of Farncombe dead?"

"Dead? Of course not! He is very much alive, and doing exceedingly good work in India."

"That is what I thought," the Marquis said as if to himself.

"Strange man, all the same. Spent most of his life in the East, and came into the title unexpectedly as the last Earl had no son."

However, the Marquis was not listening, and as Earl Bathurst stopped he asked:

"Have you ever heard in India of a man called Rowlandson?"

The Earl stared at him.

"Do you mean 'Rajah' Rowlandson?"

"'Rajah'?"

"A nickname," Earl Bathurst explained. "They tell me it is very apt because he is so rich, so important, that even the natives think of him as a Prince."

The Marquis leant forward in his chair.

"Tell me more about him."

The Earl laughed.

"That is going to take a while. He is one of those phenomena that crop up now and again and defy all the laws of average."

"In what way?"

"Well, let me think—what can I tell you about 'Rajah' Rowlandson?" Earl Bathurst asked. "He has made himself the biggest private ship-owner in the East, the biggest conveyor of cargos of all sorts and descriptions. He provides anything and everything anybody wants with a speed which leaves all his rivals gasping, and he is indispensable to the Army, the Navy, and anybody else you like to mention."

He saw the incredulous look on the Marquis's face and added:

"You looked surprised, Ardsley, and I do not blame you. But what I am telling you is the gospel truth. Rowlandson is a law unto himself, and there is nobody quite like him—or was. I suppose you know he is dead."

"I had heard that," the Marquis murmured, as the Earl was obviously expecting an answer.

"Died quite recently on the voyage home," Earl Bathurst went on. "I received the information only two days ago. It is a tragedy, a great tragedy, and God knows we have no-one to replace him."

"Do you mean to say that we used him—the British?" the Marquis queried.

"Of course we did!" Earl Bathurst replied. "If our Armis anywhere in the East wanted canons, guns, tents, or boots, Rowlandson could get them there quicker than anyone else could provide them! The East India Company, with whom he originally worked, found him invaluable."

"Who was he before he started on this strange career?" the Marquis asked.

The Earl laughed.

"You may well ask. The Rowlandsons are a distinguished and respected family in Northumberland. For generations they have gone into the County Regiment, and Rowlandson's father actually became a General! But when 'Rajah' went out to India as the Subaltern, the disorganisation and inefficiency of the ships which brought in the requirements of the troops made him start off on another career."

The Earl paused before he added:

"I believe he borrowed the money from some Indian Nabob and multiplied it a thousand times when he paid it back. Anyway, he is a man who will be greatly missed, not only by a great number of people in the East but also by ourselves."

"Do you know anything about his family," the Marquis asked, "or his relations, and where they can be found in England?"

The Earl shook his head.

"I have not the slightest idea. When I heard 'Rajah' Rowlandson was coming home, I was surprised. He has not been back for years.

There was a long silence. Then the Marquis said in a tone that was surprisingly anxious:

"Do you happen to know the name of Rowlandson's Bank?"

The Earl smiled.

"Now that is an easy question. Of course I do! It is called the Oriental-British Bank. You will find it in Lombard Street. In fact, he owns it!"

Chapter Seven

INDIRA was frightened.

Sitting in the Manager's office at the Oriental-British Bank, she found that things were not going as she had expected.

The carriage she had hired from the Livery Stable had moved depressingly slowly, but it had given her time to think out exactly what she should do. In fact, she had been turning it over and over in her mind ever since leaving Ardsley Hall.

She felt sure that the Bank Manager, who had been appointed to the Bank by her father, would be able to help her in every way and first of all to find her somewhere to stay.

She was well aware that she could not stay in an Hotel alone, and she thought perhaps he would be able to recommend some respectable woman, or perhaps even a Lady, who would take her in until such time as she could contact her relations, who again she hoped would be known to him.

However, she felt that she was constricted at every turn by the fact that her father had communicated everything he wished done in England to his Solicitors, and she knew she must have the Bank's support to help her to deal with Jacobson.

When she arrived in Lombard Street she told the carriage she had hired to wait with her luggage, and entering the Bank she asked to be taken immediately to the Manager.

There seemed at first to be some doubt as to whether he would see her. But when she gave her name, a clerk, realising who she was, bowed her obsequiously into a large, important-looking office, where the Manager was seated behind a desk.

When she looked at him, Indira felt her heart sink, for he was an Asian.

She thought it was what she might have expected, remembering that her father had always maintained that when it came to the handling of money, there were none more intelligent and quicker-brained than the Asians.

Yet she had never envisaged that the Bank Manager in England would be one, and she knew that in consequence he would be unable to help her to find suitable accommodations.

Having lived in the East so long, she knew that Asians and Europeans seldom visited one another in their private houses and it would be impossible for her to stay with one as a guest.

The Manager, having commiserated with her over her father's death, expressing most eloquently the consternation and distress it had caused in the Bank, Indira then said:

"Now, Mr. Mendi, I need your help."

"You must be well aware, Miss Rowlandson, that it will be a pleasure to help you in every possible way I can," the Manager replied.

"The first thing I want is a list of the names and addresses of my father's relatives."

The Bank Manager looked surprised before he answered:

"I am afraid I cannot help you there, Miss Rowlandson. I always understood your father directed all his personal affairs through his Solicitors, Lawson, Cruikshank and Jacobson."

"That is true," Indira replied, "but for reasons I will explain later, I do not wish to communicate with them at the moment."

"That makes things very difficult," Mr. Mendi said, "but I will certainly look in your father's files and see if there is anything in them that might be of help."

It took some time to find the files, and when they were brought in there were so many of them that Indira thought despairingly that it might be days or weeks before she had an answer to this question alone.

As she watched Mr. Mendi turn over the closely written pages, which she could see across the desk all concerned money, she began to think frantically that time was passing, and she had no idea where she could stay the night.

Mr. Mendi put down a fat file and took up another.

"I regret, Miss Rowlandson," he said in his precise manner, "that what I have here appears to be concerned only with your father's transfer of monies from one place to another, and there are no personal details of any sort."

This was what Indira was already certain he was about to say, and she was trying to formulate in her mind exactly how she should ask him where she could go when she left the Bank, when the door opened and a rather flustered-looking clerk said:

"There is a gentleman who insists on seeing you, Sir . . ."

Before he had finished the sentence, the gentleman in question, who was behind him, had pushed his way into the room.

Indira looked round indifferently, somewhat annoyed by the interruption.

Then when she saw who was there, she gave a little cry of unrepressed joy, and without thinking she jumped to her feet and ran towards the Marquis, putting out both her hands towards him.

He felt her fingers tremble in his, and he knew she was afraid in the same way she had been the first time he had touched her when she came to Ardsley Hall.

"You are . . . here!" Indira said in a low voice. "I need your . . help."

"I thought perhaps you would," the Marquis replied.

He looked down at her and for a moment it seemed as if there was no need for words, and they were speaking to each other without them.

Then the Marquis walked towards the desk and held out his hand to the Manager.

"I am the Marquis of Ardsley," he said, "and I feel that as Miss Rowlandson has just arrived in this country, she needs not only your assistance but mine as well."

Mr. Mendi bowed before he replied:

"I am finding it very difficult, My Lord, to locate the late Mr. Rowlandson's relatives, so Your Lordship's help in the matter would be very welcome."

"Surely your father's Solicitors would have their addresses?" the Marquis suggested.

Indira hesitated and to his surprise she looked embarrassed.

"It is . . . impossible for me to . . . communicate with them at the . . . moment," she said when she realised he was waiting for an answer.

"Why?" the Marquis enquired.

At that moment there was another interruption as a clerk came into the office through another door and with a word of apology went to the Manager's side to say something that only he could hear, and hand him a piece of paper.

The Marquis said quietly to Indira:

"How could you go away without telling me where you were going?"

"H-how did you . . . find me?" she parried.

"I have been to see Earl Bathurst at the Colonial Office, who told me a great deal about your father."

Indira blushed and did not look at the Marquis as she said:

"I . . . I am sorry I . . . deceived you."

The Marquis was about to reply, when Mr. Mendi interrupted by saying:

"This is very strange, and forgive me, Miss Rowlandson, but I suppose this cheque for such a large amount is signed by you?"

Indira started and took from the Manager what the clerk had just handed to him and saw that it was a cheque made out for ten thousands pounds and signed "Indira Rowlandson."

The signature was not in the least like her own and there was no need to ask who had presented it.

"It is a forgery!" she said firmly.

"A forgery?" Mr. Mendi exclaimed.

The Marquis bent forward and took the cheque from Indira's hands.

"Is the man who presented this still waiting?" he asked the clerk.

"Yes, Sir."

"Then call the Porters and have him apprehended immediately," the Marquis ordered.

The clerk looked at Mr. Mendi for confirmation and the Bank Manager nodded.

"We must certainly question him as to where he comes from and who has sent him, so do as His Lordship says."

The clerk hurried from the room and Mr. Mendi sat down again in his chair.

"Have you any idea, Miss Rowlandson," he enquired, "who could have forged this cheque?"

Indira drew in her breath and knew there was nothing she could do now but tell the truth.

*

Driving beside the Marquis in his Phaeton through the crowded streets of the city, she thought with a sense of relief which was almost overwhelming that she no longer had to be afraid.

The Marquis seemed to take over everything that concerned her in a manner which left nobody in any doubt that he was in command, and she knew it was only a question of hours before Mr. Jacobson would be imprisoned awaiting trial.

Before they left the Bank, the Marquis told Mr. Mendi that all communications relating to Mr. Rowlandson's Estate and anything that concerned his daughter were to be sent to Ardsley House in Park Lane.

As they were bowed out into Lombard Street, the Marquis's groom told the carriage Indira had hired to follow them.

The Marquis then drove in a manner which made her feel that he had taken all her burdens from her, and as in her dream she was flying up to the moon.

Since he was concentrating on his horses, they hardly spoke before they arrived in Park Lane, and as she walked across a marble Hall and into a large, comfortable Study lined with books, she felt it had the same atmosphere as the Marquis's house in the country, and it was almost as if she had come home.

He followed her into the Study and said:

"I suggest you take off your bonnet and coat. I am going to give you a glass of champagne. I feel you need it."

As he spoke with what she felt was a kinder voice than he had ever used to her before, she felt her love for him welling up inside her like a shaft of sunlight illuminating everything and sweeping away the shadows.

She had known when he came so unexpectedly into the Manager's office at the Bank that he was like an Arch-angel delivering her from her fears and difficulties, and most of all from the terror of being alone.

She told herself severely that he must never be aware how much she loved him, and that she would never behave in a possessive, over-intimate manner like Lady Sinclair and the other ladies who had fawned over him in the country.

Obediently she put her bonnet and her blue coat down on a chair and, tidying her hair with both hands, walked across the room to stand at the window looking out onto the garden which was at the back of the house.

The fragrance of the flowers in the beds, and the trees with their leaves green against the sky, made her think of the beauty of Ardsley Hall, and she said spontaneously:

"Papa told me how beautiful England was in the summer, but I was so young when I last saw it that I had forgotten."

"I am glad you think it beautiful," the Marquis replied.

He walked to her side and handed her a glass of champagne, and as she took it from him he said:

"I think we should drink a toast because this is a very special day for both of us."

She looked at him in surprise and he added:

"I have been clever enough to find you again, and as you have already said, you needed me."

"I was not . . . expecting the Manager of Papa's Bank to be an Asian. I had assumed he would be an Englishman and hoped he might invite me to . . . stay in his home until I could find . . . one of my relatives."

"You will stay here with me," the Marquis said, "and that is something I want to talk to you about."

"There is . . . something I must tell you . . . first," Indira interrupted.

"What is it?"

"Although I . . . deceived you by . . . pretending to be Lady Mary Combe . . . it was not quite so . . . wrong as it must . . . seem."

She spoke a little hesitatingly, finding it difficult to put into words that she wished to say.

Because she loved the Marquis, she could not bear him to believe that she had called herself a Lady of Title just because she was a snob.

She had not told Charles and Jimmy, but she thought now she must tell the Marquis that she had had a reason for choosing such a title.

"I am sure it is of no importance," the Marquis said, "but of course I will listen to anything you wish to tell me."

"Lady Mary Combe is my . . . cousin, and the Earl of Farncombe is my . . . uncle."

She thought the Marquis still did not understand, and she said quickly:

"Mama was his sister . . . but she died before he became so . . . important, and I knew when I . . . used Mary's name that she would not . . . mind my . . . doing so."

"I am glad you have told me," the Marquis said, "although quite frankly, it is not of the least importance. What

I really want is to be told why you minded what I thought."

"Of course I minded!" Indira said quickly. "When you have been so kind, not only when we were in the country . . . but in helping me . . . now at this . . . moment . . ."

There was a pause, then the Marquis said in a deep voice:

"Have you asked yourself why I should be so concerned about you?

The way he spoke and the fact that he was standing so near to her made Indira feel a little quiver go through her.

Because she was afraid the Marquis might become aware of her feelings, she moved away from him to the centre of the room, where she set down her glass of champagne.

The Marquis did not follow her but merely watched her, thinking that the sunlight on her hair was the most beautiful thing he had ever seen.

Unexpectedly he asked:

"Are you still afraid of me, Indira?"

"A . . . afraid?" she questioned.

"You were afraid when you arrived at Ardsley Hall," he said, "and I knew during dinner you were afraid of Wrotham. When I rescued you from him in the Library, you told me that you hated men, and yet you did not seem to be afraid of me."

He waited, until Indira said in a very low voice, as if she was tracing in her mind a sequence of events:

"You showed me your . . . Chinese poems . . . and the T'ang horse . . . and because of what . . . you said . . . everything changed."

"Everything?"

"What I had been thinking and feeling. You . . . guided and . . . inspired me."

He drew in his breath. Then slowly, as if he was still afraid he might frighten her, he walked from the window to where she was standing by a round table on which there were a number of books.

She looked not at him but at what lay on the table. As he drew near to her he knew that she quivered and he was almost sure it was not with fear.

He stood for a moment in silence before he said:

"When I received your letter on Sunday morning and thought I would never find you again, I went to the Library and took down the book of poems we had been reading. I opened it at random, Indira, and read a poem which seemed to me to be the answer to what I was feeling."

He paused, and as if Indira knew she had to make some response to what he had said, she raised her eyes slowly and, he thought, a little shyly, and then found it impossible to look away.

Softly the Marquis said:

> Kuan-kuan cry the ospreys
> On the islet in the river.
> Lovely is the good lady,
> Fit bride for our lord.

Indira did not move as he finished speaking but only waited, and he saw a sudden light come into her strange eyes.

Then as the colour rose in her cheeks like the breaking of the dawn, she made a little incoherent sound and moved towards him.

His arms went round her and she hid her face against his shoulder as he held her very close to him.

"It was a message, my darling," he said, "which I feel neither you nor I can disobey. How soon will you marry me?"

For a moment she was very still. Then almost like the rhythmic movement of the sea or the sound of music, she lifted her face to his and he found her lips.

Because he knew it was the first time she had been kissed and was afraid of reawakening her fear, he kissed her very gently, almost without passion, as one might kiss a child.

Then as he felt her whole body quiver against him, and as he knew her lips, soft and sweet, responded to his, his kiss became more insistent, more possessive.

He knew as he held her close and still closer that the feelings she aroused in him were different from any emotion he had ever known before in his whole life.

Somewhere at the back of his mind he realised that what they were feeling for each other was part of the poems they had read and of the vitality and vigour of the T'ang horses.

It was the beauty of his home and everything that he had once reached out to when he was young, then had lost when he grew older and cynical.

To Indira it was all the wonder, beauty, and glory of the East and the spiritual world she had sensed beneath it. It was inexpressible in words except when she talked with her father, and then with the Marquis.

She knew now that all her studies with her Professors, and what she had felt in the Temples and in the beauty of every country she had visited, could be expressed in one word—Love.

Only when she felt as if the Marquis had swept her up and they were riding amongst the stars did he raise his head and ask in a strangely unsteady voice:

"What do you feel about me now?"

Indira spoke what was in her heart as she said:

"I . . . love you . . . I love you! I know . . . the . . . hidden meaning of your poems . . . is my . . . love for . . . you."

The Marquis did not reply but kissed her with slow, demanding, passionate kisses until her whole body vibrated to his.

Only when the world was forgotten and they were no longer human but like gods did they come back to earth as if the strain was unendurable and for the moment they must again breathe normally.

The Marquis drew Indira to a sofa, then sat down with his arms round her.

"How can I have found you so unexpectedly, when I did not believe you even existed?"

"I never . . . thought there would be a . . . man who would . . . understand what I was . . . thinking and feeling . . . except Papa."

"We have so much to discover about each other," the Marquis said, "and as it will take us a lifetime, we must be married at once so that we need not waste an hour or a day apart when we might be together."

There was a note of passion in his voice which made Indira feel as if what he said was echoed within herself.

Then she gave a sudden little cry that was different and asked:

"Are you sure you should . . . marry me?"

"I have never been so sure of anything in my life as I am that you should be my wife."

"But . . . you do not . . . understand."

"What do I not understand?"

"That perhaps I am not the . . . right person for . . . you."

The way she spoke made the Marquis look at her penetratingly before he said:

"What are you trying to tell me?"

"If I . . . tell you the . . . truth, will you . . . promise not to be . . . angry?"

"I could never be angry with you."

"Or . . . anybody else . . . concerned with . . . me?"

His arms tightened round her and she knew perceptively that he thought she was speaking of a man and was jealous.

"No, no!" she said quickly. "It is not like . . . that. It is just that I have not told you the . . . real reason why I . . . pretended to be my cousin . . . when I came to . . . Ardsley Hall."

"Tell me now."

A little hesitatingly and shyly, she told him of the bet which Charles and Jimmy had made with each other after what they had overheard him saying in White's Club.

The Marquis did not speak, and she finished by saying:

"When they asked me to . . . help them and . . enquired as to what Papa did, I told them he was a . . . trader."

She looked up at him and now the fear was back in her eyes as she said:

"That is in fact what he was . . . and perhaps . . . because I am not . . . grand enough . . . when you think it over . . . you will not wish to . . . marry me."

The Marquis laughed, and it was a very happy sound.

"Can you really be so foolish as not to realise, my lovely one," he asked, "that if your father were a pedlar in Cheapside, or a small shop-keeper, I would still love you and still want to marry you? We have been together, my precious, in one life or another since the beginning of time, and we will be together through all eternity."

"You believe that . . . you really believe . . . that?"

"Of course I do!" the Marquis said. "Charles has won his bet, and I will tell him so when we next see him."

"And . . . you are not . . . angry with them?"

"How can I be anything but overwhelmingly grateful to the two young men who brought you to me?" the Marquis asked. "They shall be our first guests after we are married, and we will never arrange a Steeple-Chase without asking them to compete in it."

He smiled and pressed his lips against her forehead as he said:

"But of course you will beat them to the winning-post, my darling, and me as well."

"I have no wish to beat you at anything," Indira replied. "When I left Ardsley Hall on Saturday evening . . . as I drove down the drive . . . I said in my heart: 'Good-bye, my guide, my Master, my Love,' and that is what you will . . . always be to . . . me."

"Your Master?"

"I want you to . . teach me about . . . love."

She hid her face against him and whispered:

"I am very ignorant . . . about . . . that, and . . . perhaps I will . . . bore you."

The Marquis was still. In all his many passionate and fiery affairs he had never known a woman who was pure and innocent.

He thought now that nothing could be more exciting or

rapturous than to teach Indira, whom he loved with his heart and mind, the inestimable glory of love.

"I will teach you to love me, my adorable one," he said aloud, "to love me as much as I love you!"

"I love you overwhelmingly . . . already," she replied. "My love grows . . . every time I look at . . . you . . . every time you . . . touch me and . . . every time I . . . breathe."

The way she spoke made the Marquis pull her almost roughly against him and kiss her until they were both breathless. Then he said:

"We have to be sensible for the moment, my precious one. I insist that you stay here tonight, but because it would be impossible for me to get a Special Licence for us to be married before tomorrow morning, I must make some arrangements for you to be chaperoned."

"I want to be . . . alone with . . . you," Indira said impulsively.

"That is what I want too," the Marquis agreed, "and after tomorrow you will always be with me, and in my arms, my heart, my mind, and my—soul."

Indira gave a little cry as she said:

"How can you say such wonderful . . . perfect things to me? How can I have been so lucky as to find you when to escape . . . all men I wished to enter a Convent?"

The Marquis laughed, but at the same time, as if he was afraid he might have lost her, he pulled her closer to him.

"I doubt if there is a Convent in existence which could keep you away from me," he said, "and we both know, my darling one, that because we are aware of the Spiritual Force and the power that it gives us, we have a great deal to do in the world for other people. That is our *Karma*."

"That is what Papa felt," Indira replied, "and he knew it was that same force of which you have just spoken which helped him to be the success he was. He said once that when he was in difficulties or when he was in doubt, he had only to link up with it, and it never failed him."

"That is what we did when I showed you my T'ang horse," the Marquis said quietly. "It spoke to you, and my poems did the same."

Indira smiled.

"I only hope I am a . . . 'fit bride for . . . our lord'!"

"You are perfect," the Marquis declared. "And you can be sure, my beautiful little love, that in this life at any rate we will never lose each other again."

He kissed her passionately, then rose to his feet.

"I have an elderly cousin," he said, "a widow who is not particularly well off, and I know she would be only too delighted to come here for the night. She makes no secret of the fact that she waits hopefully in her small house in Chelsea, until I have need of her."

He smiled as he added:

"I am now sending for her, and will arrange for our wedding to take place in the Grosvenor Chapel, which is only round the corner, first thing in the morning."

Indira drew in her breath.

She loved the way he spoke in his usual authoritative manner. It gave her confidence and a feeling of security she had thought she had lost forever when her father died.

She knew that the two men she loved both had this self-confidence because it came not from themselves but from the inner power in which they believed.

The Marquis walked towards the door, but when he looked back he saw Indira looking at him with such an expression of love in her eyes that he merely stood still and held out his arms.

She ran to him as if she were a homing-pigeon, and he held her close against him to look down into her face, thinking that he had never seen anybody look so radiantly happy.

"Is it true?" she asked. "Or am I . . . dreaming that you . . . love me and your T'ang horse will . . . fly us to the . . . moon?"

"I think we are on our way there already," the Marquis said, "and after we are married and you are mine completely, my darling, we will live in a very special Heaven which every man longs for but few find."

He kissed her as he finished speaking, and Indira thought it would be impossible to know an ecstasy and rapture that was greater than what she felt already.

Then, as if he forced himself to leave her, the Marquis said:

"Go and change, my beautiful bride-to-be, and when I have made all the arrangements for our future happiness, we will have tea together in the room where my mother always sat when she and my father were alone."

"I would love . . . that."

She paused before she added very softly:

"I know without your telling me that your father and mother must have loved each other . . . very much to have . . . produced anybody as . . . wonderful as you, and perhaps . . . one day . . . that is what we . . . shall be able to . . . say about . . . our children."

The way she spoke brought the fire into the Marquis's eyes. At the same time, it made him feel as if she were something sacred and he should kneel in front of her.

As he kissed her he knew that this was just the beginning of their happiness, and that Indira was right when she said that because their children would be born of love they too would have the power of linking up with the Spiritual Force as they were able to do.

"I love you!" he said with his lips and in his heart, and he knew that the love pulsating through both of them and which made them already one person was also Divine.

This was what he had always sought without really knowing it, and to Indira it was even more simple.

The T'ang horse had carried them to the moon in a dream which had become reality and from which neither of them would ever wake.